the **THREE FATES** OF **HENRIK NORDMARK**

CHRISTOPHER
MEADES

the THREE
FATES OF
HENRIK
NORDMARK

ECW PRESS

Published by ECW Press
2120 Queen Street East, Suite 200, Toronto, Ontario, Canada M4E 1E2
416.694.3348 / info@ecwpress.com

LIBRARY AND ARCHIVES CANADA CATALOGUING IN PUBLICATION

Meades, Christopher
The three fates of Henrik Nordmark / Christopher Meades.

ISBN 978-1-55022-972-1

I. Title.

PS8626.E234T47 2010   C813'.6   C2010-901255-0

Editor: Jennifer Hale
Cover Design: David Gee
Text Design: Tania Craan
Cover Images © Brent Nelson/iStockphoto.com (man);
© Xiangdong Li/iStockphoto.com (plum)
Typesetting: Mary Bowness
Production: Troy Cunningham
Printing: Webcom   1   2   3   4   5

This book is set in Akzidenz Grotesk and Garamond.

The first draft of the *Three Fates of Henrik Nordmark* was shortlisted for the 2007 International 3 Day Novel competition. In addition, excerpts of this novel have appeared in the following literary print journals:

The Feathertale Review (Toronto, Ontario)
Inch (Durham, North Carolina)
Cause & Effect (California)
Hacksaw Arts Magazine (Vancouver, BC)
The Delinquent (London, UK)

  Mixed Sources
Product group from well-managed forests, controlled sources and recycled wood or fiber
www.fsc.org Cert no. SW-COC-002358
© 1996 Forest Stewardship Council
FSC

 ANCIENT FOREST ™
FRIENDLY

The publication of *The Three Fates of Henrik Nordmark* has been generously supported by the Canada Council for the Arts which last year invested $20.1 million in writing and publishing throughout Canada, by the Ontario Arts Council, by the Government of Ontario through Ontario Book Publishing Tax Credit, by the OMDC Book Fund, an initiative of the Ontario Media Development Corporation, and by the Government of Canada through the Canada Book Fund.

 Canada Council Conseil des Arts
for the Arts du Canada   Canadä  ONTARIO ARTS COUNCIL
CONSEIL DES ARTS DE L'ONTARIO

PRINTED AND BOUND IN CANADA

ECW PRESS
ecwpress.com

To Wendy

Thanks to:

Wendy Meades, for believing in me, supporting the dream and baking me dozens of Smarties cookies before each marathon writing session.

Hanna and Claire, my two little girls. Daddy loves you . . . now try to be good.

Brian "Bear" Simmers, my best friend of 20 years.

Jen Hale, my editor, for her invaluable insight and for truly being great to work with.

The staff at ECW for all of their hard work.

Melissa Edwards and everyone at the 3 Day Novel contest who shortlisted the first draft of *Henrik Nordmark.*

Angie Kruger for her legal help & advice.

Angie Hirata for her enthusiasm and encouragement.

Mom and Dad for paying for an English Lit degree (even though it was probably against their better judgment).

Joan Witty and Anne Craig for reading every single story I ever sent them.

Margaret Helsdon, my mother-in-law, for her astonishing typo-catching abilities.

Sandra and Dan Murray for their guidance and support in the early '90s.

Katherine Dewan & the Dewan Family.

Max and Pedro.

one

Until that fateful day, Henrik Nordmark had always been an entirely unremarkable fellow. He spoke in a monotonous, repetitive drone. His conversation was benign. He thought only nondescript thoughts and had no particular ambitions in life. To those around him, he was unnoticeable, camouflaged entirely by his blandness. Henrik worked as a security guard in an office building where for twenty years he had not encountered a single incident that required him to pull out his nightstick. He stood by the doorway all day every day, sphinx-like in contrition and advancement, smiling hesitantly and being constantly ignored. You couldn't blame the people who walked by. Henrik had no redeemable features to draw one's eye. They passed him as one would pass faded wallpaper in an old hallway during an increasingly urgent search for a toilet.

Henrik didn't do anything.

He had no hobbies, no particularly close friends or interesting relatives.

His outward physical appearance resembled Alfred Hitchcock, with his bald head and stout demeanor, his double chin and the slight waddle in his walk. The only features that distinguished Henrik at all from the great filmmaker were a severe redness to his skin and a pair of Wookiee-like sideburns that book-ended his round, bulbous head, making the shadow of his skull look like an oversized grapefruit being squished in a vice.

Not even Henrik's sideburns could set him apart in a crowd. He was neither young nor old, weak nor strong; not fat enough to be obese, but chubby enough that parts of his sides folded over onto the seat next to him on the bus. He smelled a little, but his musty odor — part mildew, part inside-of-a-reptile-cage — wasn't particularly malicious and rarely did it cause great offense. Henrik had no interesting stories to tell. He'd never run through the streets in the middle of the night in a desperate search for condoms or had a girlfriend force him into a sunflower costume for Halloween. In fact, he'd never had a romantic relationship of any kind. Henrik had lived his entire forty-two years in complete obscurity. He was the weed sprouting out of the wallflower; generic in his generality.

Henrik loathed being ordinary. His whole life he'd wished for just one unique characteristic, one thing about himself that was different from the norm. For a long time, Henrik hoped that some imaginary force would miraculously intervene and make him special. During his teenage years, he waited for fate to strike. It never did. One morning in high school, a beautiful young girl with ashen hair and a bright smile accidentally mistook Henrik's locker for her own. Henrik approached the girl as she tried to enter her combination into his lock. He mumbled a vague remark about the unbridled clout of destiny and how it must have brought them together on this day. The pretty young girl looked at him as though she might become physically ill and moved three lockers to the left. Henrik knew then and there that fate would never be on his side, no matter how much he rallied for it to come his way.

In his twenties and thirties, Henrik turned his attention to karma. He tried opening doors for little old ladies and giving up his seat to people on the bus. One evening, he took off his jacket and threw it over a puddle for women to cross, thinking himself a modern-day Fred Astaire. The women on the street corner gave him a confused look and then stepped around the jacket-covered puddle before hurrying off in the opposite direction. Henrik wouldn't accept that chivalry was dead; he increased his efforts tenfold. The next painful sacrifice he made was allowing a woman who came into the pizza parlor after him to take his place in line — only to watch her order the last slice of Szechwan chicken pizza: the very slice Henrik had been dreaming of all morning, the one with the pea pods and the red pepper, the one he had taken two buses in the sweltering heat to purchase. Dumbfounded and heartbroken, Henrik ordered a slice of monotonous pepperoni and watched as the woman took three bites before brazenly tossing her slice into a nearby garbage can. Henrik would have broken into tears had he any to shed. For years, he'd tried to twist the arm of karma but it would never bend into submission. This ruthlessly discarded slice of pizza was the final straw. Karma, Henrik decided, was merely a random phrase that surly baristas wrote on tip jars in order to grossly inflate their hourly wage.

Henrik gave up on karma and fate. It was quite a serious undertaking to believe in either of these concepts wholeheartedly and without skepticism. He simply didn't have it in him to do so. The challenge was too great and the results had alternated between nonexistent and counterintuitive in every way. Everything he'd learned over the years told Henrik that he was destined to live a life unnoticed in the background. It was in the very nature of his design.

At age thirty-seven, Henrik made the optimistic assumption that perhaps his surroundings had something to do with the sheer banality of his life. He packed a bag containing two pairs of underpants, one toothbrush, a half-used jar of surprisingly ineffective Rogaine and three packages of dental floss, then walked to the train station and asked to purchase a ticket on the next train to another city.

"Which city?" the woman at the counter said.

"Any city," Henrik said, full of pride over his spontaneity.

The woman frowned in general vexation and handed him a ticket to a city 200 miles away. Henrik climbed on the train with a smile brimming from ear to ear. During the three-hour journey, that smile steadily shrank until it formed a short, agonized grimace covering just a fraction of his face. Henrik couldn't believe what he'd done. He wasn't ready for this. Nothing in his life had prepared him for new surroundings. And what if his surroundings weren't the issue at all? What if this new city proved him to be equally as boring as he'd been in his hometown? Or worse — what if it was overflowing with wide-eyed charlatans and eccentric oddballs? Henrik would shrink even farther into life's background, overshadowed by their colorful personalities and individual distinctiveness. No, he couldn't take it getting much worse. With every mile he traveled away from home, he felt more uniformly generic than he'd been the mile before. Henrik asked the conductor whether the train would eventually return to his hometown. The conductor confirmed the current route was round-trip, but that Henrik would have to purchase a return ticket at the next stop.

As the train arrived at the station, Henrik planned to

scurry out and buy a ticket and then return as quickly as he could to the confines of his car. He made his way toward the door but was so terrified of what he might find outside that he hid himself in a custodial closet reeking of industrial soap. He sat amongst the filthy mops and grimy toilet plungers until the train finally returned home, at which point Henrik made a mad dash from the train doors, jumped face first onto the concrete and kissed it like some B-level Hollywood actor would kiss sand to express his undying love for the land in which he was born.

Only Henrik didn't love his home. It was merely the lesser of two evils. He would never try to leave again. He simply didn't have the gumption to start a new life. Henrik returned to his post as security guard at the office building and lived a life of monotony, secretly wishing that he would someday be unique, yet knowing his dreams would never come true. Henrik lived five more years in life's background.

Until one morning when he went to the market to purchase some plums.

On the infamous morning in question, Henrik waddled along the street in better spirits than usual. Earlier that day he had sat down on the toilet to rid himself of a particularly troublesome blueberry muffin. His bowels were free. It was a quite joyous sensation to be walking down the street two pounds lighter and he was looking forward to purchasing some plums. He'd always enjoyed the taste of plums — apples and oranges be damned — and his Tuesday trip to the market was often the highlight of his week. Henrik entered the market as he normally did and said hello to the cashier. The cashier grunted in acknowledgment but didn't look up from his stack of receipts. Henrik walked through the store and surveyed the fruit. The papayas looked plump and slightly orange, as though they'd just arrived and come into season. Their big brothers the bananas were slightly worse off, with a few scattered brown liver spots covering their torsos. He rounded the entire store, past the nearly ripe peaches and the forgotten raspberries, before returning to the front where the plums were located beside the cashier's desk. Keenly, Henrik leaned over and selected three of the most delicious-looking morsels. He tucked them under his arm and selected three more.

As Henrik picked up the sixth plum, fate struck. His fingers gripped the plum precariously, like the three-pronged claw of an arcade machine clenching a stuffed animal. Henrik increased his grip to keep it from dropping. Ripe and bursting with juice, the plum's skin ruptured without warning and sent a wild spurt of liquid up into Henrik's eye. Henrik dropped the plums and recoiled in agony. He turned around and crashed into a man and a woman, both of whom were purchasing lottery tickets from the cashier. The woman slipped on a tiny puddle of plum juice, forcing the young man to catch her. Amidst the chaos, the cashier flew into a rage and began berating all three of them.

Henrik immediately felt embarrassed. He picked up five plums and set them on the counter. His eyes searched for the sixth plum. It had rolled along the ground, toward the entrance and out through the doorway where it was gathering momentum on the sidewalk, heading toward the street. Henrik darted outside and valiantly chased the renegade plum. He was about to leap into the street when a stranger grabbed him by the arms, saving him from diving headlong into oncoming traffic and most certain death.

Henrik faced his savior. It was a man in a black tuxedo.

"Thank you," he said.

"You must be careful, my friend," the man in the tuxedo said.

Henrik couldn't help but stare at the man. With his neatly combed hair and formal attire, the man in the tuxedo appeared to be quite the international man of mystery. How strange it was for him to be dressed this way so early in the morning.

From across the street, two shadowy figures were watching from a car with darkened windows. They saw the descent of the plums and a great kerfuffle take place around the lottery booth, then watched the man save Henrik's life. In rapid fashion, they unrolled a window and extended an old-fashioned camera. The man in the tuxedo sensed danger and bent over to pick up the plum for Henrik. The camera's flash went off. It was so strong the bulb broke and smoke gasped from the tiny pieces of shattered glass.

"Was this what you were so desperate to find?" The man in the tuxedo handed Henrik the lost plum as the car squealed its tires and took off down the street. Flummoxed by the brightness of the flash, Henrik nodded his head and took the plum in his hand. The man in the tuxedo turned and left the scene, never to be heard from again.

Henrik brought the plum back into the store where the cashier and the two people he'd bumped into were still sorting out the mess. Both customers had finished filling out their lottery tickets but couldn't figure out whose was whose or which was which. The cashier, displeased with the whole situation, grabbed the tickets, ran them through his machine and handed one to the woman and the other to the young man. The young man tucked his in the back pocket of his jeans and apologized, then left quickly. The woman placed hers in her purse and shook her head before storming out the doors. Sheepishly, Henrik paid for the plums and exited the store. He rounded the corner and left the marketplace behind.

As the shock wore off, Henrik reflected on his near-death experience. A nagging thought burdened him as he walked down the sidewalk. Like a tick slowly burrowing to the forefront of Henrik's skull, it gnawed away at his brain. Were it not for that stranger in the tuxedo, he might have died back there in the street. Henrik's reflection grew into a realization, burgeoned rapidly into comprehension and dove headfirst along the path to awareness. He stopped in the middle of the sidewalk, plagued with the notion that he could have died this morning without ever being unique, without ever having a defining characteristic for which he would be remembered. He wondered what they would say at his funeral. Moreover, who would even attend such an event? Henrik maintained little contact with his extended family and his mother's agoraphobia had kept her as a shut-in since the mid-nineties. She wouldn't be there. His employer might make an appearance. That Jamaican woman who worked the night shift at his office building. She might attend. Or she might not. She rarely acknowledged him and had out-and-out ignored his suggestion that their two-person department have a Secret Santa program last Christmas. Henrik racked his brain for who else would attend. He could think of no one. There was not one single soul on this green Earth who he could be absolutely certain would take the time to attend his funeral and Henrik couldn't even blame them. The poor person giving his eulogy would have nothing to say. Henrik himself would probably fall asleep at a ceremony so boring.

He stomped his feet on the sidewalk.

"Enough," he said underneath his breath. He said it again and again. The word swelled in volume until it reached a crescendo. "Enough. Enough! ENOUGH!" Henrik picked the fatal plum from his bag. It was covered in street grime. He tossed the plum into a nearby garbage bin and listened to it splat atop the other refuse. Standing in front of an Asian foot massage parlor, Henrik had an epiphany. He would turn his life around. He would find something interesting about himself.

He would become unique if it killed him.

 two

The man in the red suit entered the retirement home carrying an envelope full of money in his breast pocket and a
briefcase loaded with weaponry in his right hand. He
approached the reception desk and asked to speak to
Conrad. The woman behind the counter stared long and
hard at the young man's bright red suit, his slicked-back hair
and the brazen bravado on his face. She'd heard rumors that
this kind of man had visited Conrad in the past. Briefly, she
considered calling the retirement home director or better yet
the police, before reluctantly leading the man in the red suit
down a corridor and up a flight of stairs. She opened the
door to the large music room.

Inside, fifty seniors were singing in chorus. The sound
was ghastly. Most of the seniors merely muttered the words
while a few shrill old ladies belted them out as though they
were debuting at Carnegie Hall. The only reason the residents attended the singing hour at all was because the music
teacher had a friend in the kitchen and each of them feared
the unhygienic things that could happen to their string beans
were they to skip a session. The teacher was cruel in her song
selections, forgoing the classics in favor of the more contem-
porary, booty-shaking tracks of today in which the elderly
were forced to chant phrases like "shake that ass" and "lovely
lady lumps." They'd just finished a listless rendition of

Rihanna's "Umbrella" when the man in the red suit entered.

"I'm here to see Conrad," he said.

The seniors looked over and stared at the man in the red suit. A nearsighted, expectant grandmother even approached him in the hope that it was her grandson before being turned away by the young man's scowl.

Standing in the center of the room, the music teacher had no patience for visitors. "And a-one and a-two . . ." she called out. The piano started up again and the ivories chimed out the first three bars of Eamon's "I Don't Want You Back." The seniors turned to face the group and joined in halfway through the first verse.

From the back, three shadowy figures stood up from their folding chairs.

A smile pursed Conrad's lips. He walked towards the man in the red suit, a cane assisting him as he moved. Alfred and Billy Bones followed.

"Is there someplace we can talk in private?" the man in the red suit said.

Five minutes later the four of them were alone in a room down the hall. The man in the red suit stared at the three old geezers sitting on the faded davenport in front of him. Conrad looked exactly as the stories said he would. He was dressed in all black, with a thin moustache curled at the ends and a full, thick head of hair. His face belied his ninety years, with purplish swags under his eyes and a subtle gray hue to his flesh. He was wearing, of all things, a crimson-lined cape, which gave him the pretense of a dramatic stage villain. He spoke with an English accent — faked for decades, of course — and maintained an air of quiet confidence about him. The other two, with their worn three-piece brown suits and massive, distracting wrinkles, looked like Statler and Waldorf, the two old men who heckled the Muppets from the comfort of their balcony seats. Billy Bones was the short fat one. Alfred was tall and skinny.

"There has been some concern on the part of my employers that you might not be able to complete this task," the man in the red suit said.

"Nonsense." Conrad dismissed him with a wave of his hand.

"There's been talk about your advanced age," the man said. "There are rumors of epilepsy."

"Leprosy?" Billy Bones yelled.

"No, epilepsy."

"There ain't been no leprosy since the turn of the century," Billy said.

"That's not what I said."

"That *is* what you said, son."

The man in the red suit looked perplexed.

"Admit it!" Billy Bones slapped his armrest.

"There are concerns about this one's hearing," the man pointed to Billy Bones. "And this one can't speak," he motioned toward Alfred.

"That's not true," Alfred mouthed without emitting a sound.

"I assure you — none of us has epilepsy," Conrad said.

"My great-aunt had leprosy," Billy Bones said. "It's a hell of a way to die."

"We are quite capable of completing the task before us," Conrad said.

"You check the halls for fingers falling off — that's how you spot leprosy. They leave 'em behind in their haste, they do," Billy Bones said. His sentence drifted off into doddering laughter.

The man in the red suit closed his eyes and sighed.

"Did you bring everything?" Conrad said.

The man reached into his breast pocket and produced an envelope.

"Hand it to my associate," Conrad said.

Alfred took the envelope full of hundred-dollar bills and tucked it inside his jacket. The man flipped open his briefcase. Conrad didn't even glance at its contents. He waited until the man in the red suit set the case down on the coffee table. "And the target," he said. "Did you bring a picture of the target?"

From his jacket, the man pulled out a second envelope containing a single photograph and handed it to Alfred.

"We'll be in touch," Conrad stood up to shake the man's hand. The man in the red suit put out his hand and when he did, Conrad grabbed it and pulled him in close. "Do not make the mistake of letting my old age fool you, young man. I am the most dangerous chap you will ever meet."

The man in the red suit tried to pull his hand away but couldn't. Conrad was surprisingly strong.

"I'm sure you've heard the old stories," Conrad said.

"Yes sir," the man said.

"Then you know how many men I've killed."

He squeezed the man's hand hard.

"Two hundred." The man's fingers crunched under Conrad's iron grip.

"Two hundred and twelve," Conrad said. "So you'd best clean that smug look off your face before I do it for you."

"Yes sir," the man said.

Conrad released his hand and the man backed away.

"Your employers will hear from us when the job is done," he said.

The man in the red suit exited the room and stormed down the hallway. He climbed into his car and drove away from the retirement home as quickly as he could, shaking his head. He couldn't believe his bosses had chosen these three. One of them was deaf and the other was a mute. The only reason he had any faith in them at all was Conrad. "At least there's nothing wrong with the leader," the man in the red suit said as he pulled onto the highway. He picked up his cell phone and called his bosses.

"The package has been delivered."

"Do you have faith that they can do the job?" the voice on the other end said.

The man in the red suit thought about the pain searing through his arm and the numbness that had yet to subside in his fingers. "Yes," he said.

Back in the retirement home, the three associates were still sitting on the same couch with the items lined up in a row on the coffee table. Conrad reached forward and felt the objects inside the briefcase. He groped to the side and ran his fingers along the edges of the cold hard cash. The photograph stared back at his glassy, blind eyes. Conrad sat up and waited. A few seconds passed before he smacked Alfred on the arm. "Eventually one of you is going to have to tell me what we have here."

Billy Bones spoke up.

"The case has everything we asked for. Are you sure you remember how to use these things?"

"Of course I'm sure. Now what else is there?"

"The money's all here. Forty thousand dollars in hundreds."

"And the target?"

Billy Bones stuttered a little.

Alfred tried to speak. Conrad and Billy edged in close to where they could feel his breath on their skin: "Alfred Hitchcock." He pointed to the picture, taken outside the local marketplace. Standing in front of a blurred-out man in a tuxedo was a startled-looking Henrik Nordmark.

 three

Later that morning the young man from the lottery kiosk entered the third floor of a brand new office tower down-town for the biggest job interview of his life. Roland breathed in deep. The entire building, from its dark red window blinds to the plush chairs in the lobby, smelled like the inside of a new car. He had long since changed from his jeans into his best suit. He'd even shaved his face and ironed his clothes for the big day.

Roland worked in a cubicle at the other end of town in a mind-numbing but more often than not tolerable office job in which he created periodical reports that he was pretty sure no one ever read. Recently management had unveiled a new company ambassador, television star Regis Philbin, who appeared in company-produced videos wearing a shiny *Who Wants to Be a Millionaire?* tie and promoting the new com-pany mantra: What Would Regis Do? Roland had seen at least six of these videos and in each of them, a youthful-looking employee with a slightly befuddled gaze behind his eyes (and always carrying a file folder) would be faced with a moral dilemma, at which point Regis would pop seemingly out of nowhere to provide an answer that was equal parts ethically unimpeachable and difficult to argue with. Roland could hardly go a day at work without someone asking him what Regis would do.

Today he had an interview to be the new special assistant to the International Vice President in charge of Employee Relations. The job involved travel to all manner of exotic locations and every kind of perk one could imagine: great food, a company expense account, and most importantly, the opportunity to escape the dreary doldrums of his gray cubicle walls.

Two days ago, Roland and his cubicle neighbor Mason spotted a confidential job posting on their supervisor's desk and decided to apply without telling anyone. Their company outsourced the interview to a human resources company on the other side of town. The whole meeting had a clandestine air about it and Roland stole quietly through the hallways until he reached the office.

As he entered, Roland saw Mason sitting in the waiting room.

"Are you at 10:30?" Roland said.

"Yep. How about you?"

"I'm right after you." Roland sat down beside Mason. He looked down to see a hint of white athletic socks edging out underneath Mason's wool pant-leg. Roland smiled.

When they first started working together, Mason had seemed cool. Over time, however, things slowly turned sour. In the four years Roland had known him, Mason had done some things under the guise of friendship that Roland considered to be, while not blatantly immoral, downright despicable.

Mason started by placing an open case of sardines in Roland's desk drawer.

A week after the smell died down, Mason switched the letters on Roland's computer by prying them out with a pair of scissors and jamming them back in. When Roland sat down at his computer to start the day, he looked at his keyboard and instead of typing his regular password, he typed in a vile curse word that was equal parts sexist and racist. He entered the same password over and over again, all the while staring at the keyboard thinking that something was horribly wrong. Roland speculated that he might be having a flashback to his college days when he smoked way too much pot. Or perhaps he was suffering a slight stroke.

He called the company help desk and told the lady who answered that his password wasn't working. She used her computer to connect to Roland's desktop and decode the asterisks Roland had typed in.

"Is this some dirty joke?"

Roland insisted it wasn't.

The help desk lady fell suddenly silent and her voice took on a clipped, even hostile tone.

In the next cubicle, Mason laughed like a hyena until he couldn't take it anymore. He came over, pried the keys out of Roland's keyboard and placed them back where they belonged while Roland apologized profusely to the offended help desk employee.

The incident with the keyboard turned out to be only a single drop in the bucket compared to the ocean of cruel trickery that followed.

A short while later, Mason convinced Roland to join him in a beard growing contest. The rules were simple. Each participant had to grow a beard for one full year. Shaving of the neck was permissible but any trimming, tidying, un-natting, or shaping in any way with a sharp metallic device was strictly prohibited. The participant with the longest beard at the end of the year would be taken for lunch by his vanquished opponent. Mason suggested the contest with unbridled enthusiasm and even described the lunch as a "pizza party." Roland thought it was a great idea and immediately stopped shaving. Mason, for his part, didn't shave either.

A week later Mason was sent on a work assignment to southern Florida for five months. While he was gone, a wolf-man-like plague of patches grew on Roland's face. Black and orange and ugly, the beard sprouted from his face like untamed weeds, focusing primarily on the right corner of his chin while neglecting the upper left moustache region entirely. Roland had to endure inquisitive looks bordering on aversion from his coworkers as well as random catcalls from people on the street.

It would all be worth it, even the severe itching, Roland decided, if he won that pizza party. Sure, Mason would also get to eat the pizza. But he would have to pay for it and free pizza from a vanquished opponent always tastes better than pizza you have to pay for.

Mason and Roland had been trading barbs over email for months, bragging as to the various aspects of their beards — length, fullness, mean average bristle count. At the end of the fifth month, Mason returned from his work assignment. Roland hurried in to work to compare beards, only to discover Mason sitting in his chair, bright-eyed, tanned . . . and clean-shaven. When Mason saw Roland's beard, he broke out laughing. Mason had never grown a beard. It had all been part of an elaborate — and quite successful — ruse to make Roland look like the office lunatic.

Mason wondered out loud why Roland wasn't laughing.

"Come on," he said. "Everyone appreciates a good burn."

Roland did not appreciate the burn.

In mock friendship, Mason offered to still pay for their pizza party. Devastated, Roland couldn't bring himself to accept the invitation.

Roland looked at Mason in his suit and tie, sitting beside him in the waiting room of the interviewer's office.

"How are you doing?" Roland said.

"I'm sore. I played Ultimate last night."

"Ultimate?"

"Yeah, it's a new sport. My legs are really sore from playing."

Roland had never heard of Ultimate before. What was this new sport that Mason had been playing? If they called it "Ultimate," it must be something pretty awesome. Roland's mind swirled with all of the possibilities. Perhaps it was some variation on kickboxing. Or jousting. Or a brand of dodgeball played above a flaming pit in which the competitors are enclosed in a cage and the spectators are permitted, within reason of course, to poke the opposing team with sticks, or better yet, knives. It must be a really tough sport for Mason to deem it the ultimate sport of them all.

"What's involved in this Ultimate?"

"You catch a Frisbee, you throw it to someone else, and then you run and catch it again."

"That's it?"

"Yeah, it's like the toughest game you could ever play."

"Really?" Roland said.

"Yes, really."

"Do you play it against giant men who threaten to tackle you?"

"No. It's co-ed. And there's no tackling."

"Then why do they call it Ultimate?"

Mason rolled his eyes. "They used to call it Ultimate Frisbee. But the Frisbee brand name is trademarked by some big corporation who threatened to sue. So the league organizers shortened it to Ultimate."

"That name's a little misleading, don't you think?"

"How so?"

"Well, when you said 'Ultimate,' I immediately started thinking about all of these insane, American Gladiator–type games you might be competing in. But you're just running around throwing a Frisbee."

"You don't understand," Mason said. "It's a really hard game."

"Oh, I believe you. But is it the *ultimate* game? Wouldn't hockey or football or Greco-Roman wrestling be a better candidate to be called the ultimate sport?"

Mason shook his head. "You'll never understand until you play it yourself."

"Maybe I should. Can I join your team?"

"No. We're only looking for girls right now."

Roland turned away and stared at the corner of the room. Mason shook his head again and busied himself by reading a three-year-old copy of the *New Yorker* on the coffee table until Roland spoke.

"You got your hair cut," he said.

"Yep," Mason ran his hand through his hair. It was short on the sides with an angular poof on top.

"How much did that run you?"

"Eight bucks at Magic Cuts. They gave me a hot dog and a pop too. No extra charge."

"Wow. It looks good." Roland's tone dripped with sarcasm but Mason didn't seem to pick up on it. He had put down the copy of the *New Yorker* and was busy flipping through an issue of *Golf Digest*.

"Do you see this guy?" Mason pointed to a middle-aged golfer in a striped shirt on the cover. "He was a golf instructor for years until about eight months ago when he made the big time. He played in his first major golf tournament and won the whole thing. The prize money was something like eight million bucks. Then he traded up big time."

Roland faced Mason for the first time since they sat down.

"What do you mean?"

"The golf pro made millions and the first thing he did was divorce his wife so he could marry a Victoria's Secret model, you know, kind of like what Lance Armstrong did when he divorced his first wife to date Sheryl Crow."

"People really do this?"

"It happens all the time," Mason said.

"Really?" Roland said.

"Really."

Roland undid his suit jacket and sat there lost in thought. Two minutes passed in silence before the door to the interviewer's office opened. Out walked a gruff old man in an expensive tight-fitting suit. He had a round belly and his face was all eyebrows and Coke-bottle glasses. "Mason, you're next," he said.

They shut the door behind them. For fifteen minutes, Roland picked at the rubber on the sole of his shoe until Mason came out. Both men were all smiles as they exited the interview room. They shook hands, patted each other on the shoulder and even shared a laugh. The interviewer gave Mason a gentle slap on his shoulder and flexed the bicep on his right arm. Roland was surprised to see Mason reach up and feel the man's bulging muscle.

The interviewer looked at Roland. "Let me hit the bathroom and then we'll talk," he said.

Roland waited until he left the room.

"What was that all about?" he said.

Mason hesitated. "It was the strangest thing," he said. "I've never seen anything like it. The interview was going really well until about the ten-minute mark when the guy challenged me to arm wrestle."

"Really?"

"Really. I told him I didn't want to arm wrestle and that we should talk about the job. But he wouldn't take no for an answer. He said he doesn't respect a man without the gumption to arm wrestle him and that he'd never hire a man he doesn't respect."

"So what did you do?"

"I arm wrestled him."

"Right there in the meeting room?"

Mason nodded. "Yep."

"Did you win?"

"No," Mason's voice changed. "That old guy's really strong. He beat me in three seconds flat. When it was over I asked him if I got the job and he said no. He said he might have given it to me if I'd had the guts to challenge him to arm wrestle and not the other way around."

Roland looked at the office; his eyes drifted down the hallway where the interviewer had gone to the washroom.

"What should I do?"

Mason glanced back at the office door. "If it were me, if I had to do it all over again," he said, "I would walk right in there and challenge him before he even had the chance to challenge me. That would show him you have balls of steel. He would hire you for sure if you did that."

Roland churned his jaw and squinted a little.

"I don't know," he said.

"It's up to you." Mason walked toward the exit. "I already know I'm not getting the job. If I were you, I'd do everything in my power to show this guy you mean business." Mason left the interview area. The room was quiet for a few seconds before the interviewer returned from the washroom.

Roland immediately started sizing up the man's forearms.

"Let's get this over with, shall we?" the man said.

From the moment they entered the office and sat down around a small table, this man's demeanor told Roland he had absolutely no chance of getting the job. Roland swore he could see the man's eyes turn upwards and to the left — a classic characteristic of deceit. He also noticed the man's arms were limp and that he only looked Roland in the mouth and jaw, not in the eyes. This man was completely disinterested and had no intention of hiring him. Roland felt a twinge of panic in his chest. When the man spoke, all of Roland's fears were realized.

"So, tell me about yourself," he said.

This was an unqualified catastrophe. The man drawled out the word *So* as if he didn't even want to start the conversation, as though he was thinking inane thoughts about breakfast and bacon and pancakes. The way he enunciated the word *me* was even worse. He broke sharp at the M and spent very little time on the E — the hallmark indication of apathy toward a self-referencing pronoun. This was bad. Very bad. The interview was barely eight seconds old and already it was an out-of-control locomotive steaming off the tracks. Roland had to do something to right its course.

The thought popped into his head: What would Regis do?

He placed his elbow firmly on the table and lifted his hand up in a 45-degree angle. "Let's arm wrestle," Roland said. "You and me. We'll see which one of us is the real man here."

Silence.

The interviewer's eyes grew wide. His expression morphed from ambivalence to confusion and then outrage, all in the course of a few seconds. Meanwhile, Roland's arm hovered precariously in the air. The interviewer took off his glasses and locked eyes with Roland.

"Boy — what in hell do you think you're doing?"

Roland's arm deflated to the table.

"But . . . but I saw you flexing your bicep. Mason reached out and touched it."

The interviewer leaned forward. He seemed to be growing angrier with each passing second. "That young man and I work out at the same gym," he said.

Despite pleading with the man and practically begging for a second chance, Roland was ushered out the door and into the street. He mumbled to himself and replayed the embarrassing incident in his head. Could anything have been more humiliating? More demoralizing? Mason was going to get the big promotion and travel around the world while Roland was destined to live out his days in his dreary gray cubicle. And he wouldn't just have to share it with Mason, who for all his ill wit and bad haircut was a diabolical trickster, but most likely with someone even more crafty and cunning. Roland groaned out loud and headed back to the office.

At the time, he could have never known that the very next day, his fortunes would change.

four

Bonnie, the woman Henrik bumped into at the lottery booth, left the marketplace and entered the apartment building three doors down from the market: a home she shared with her husband Clyde. Ten years ago when they met, Bonnie and Clyde were immediately taken with one another when they realized their names matched those of the famous movie couple. They based their entire relationship on this interesting, if somewhat irrelevant, coincidence. To Bonnie, it wasn't just coincidence but rather a twist of fate. She fell in love with Clyde because the moon and the stars above told her to fall in love with him. Over the past decade, she'd gradually become disillusioned with Clyde's rampant gambling and his womanizing ways. Moreover, he had an outright disrespect for her job. Bonnie's job was of the utmost importance to her. Her parents and friends supported her. She couldn't understand why her husband didn't support her.

From their wedding day, Bonnie's love for Clyde deteriorated. Very quickly, she started to dislike him. This dislike developed rapidly into severe loathing. Twelve months ago, Bonnie phoned her parents up in tears. She wanted a divorce and she wanted them to pay for it. She couldn't live with this man anymore. Not for another day. Bonnie was shocked when her father not only refused to pony up the cash, he insisted no daughter of his would be getting a divorce. "Not within my lifetime," her father said. "We might forgive your lifestyle and accept some of the choices you've made, but you made a commitment to that young man and we expect you to live up to your obligations." Bonnie pleaded with him, cried for hours, and when that didn't work she appealed to his logical nature. Bonnie's father wouldn't budge. The right and left sides of his brain were in equal parts resolved. Bonnie couldn't litigate her way out of this in a courtroom filled with attorneys and statutes and men in suits.

So, for close to a year, Bonnie had been trying to kill her husband. She would place arsenic in his soup and even left a tuberculosis-infected needle she snagged from the hospital under his pillow. Despite her best efforts, Bonnie's attempts always fell short of their mark. True, Clyde had gotten sick a few times. And there was a promising three-week stay in the hospital a few months ago. That showed some real potential. But as time went by, she started to believe that Clyde was entirely indestructible. She couldn't kill him no matter how hard she tried and his resilience brought her to a state of misery and despair. Lately, she'd suspected Clyde knew she was attempting to kill him and had been using his wiles to avoid being murdered.

Clyde, for his part, was completely oblivious to the fact that Bonnie was trying to kill him. He'd been far too busy trying to kill her to notice. Clyde wanted his wife dead for an entirely different set of reasons. Over time, the years had faded on Bonnie. Her beauty, incalculable in her youth, had curdled like warm milk left in the afternoon sun. Though she had once been glamorous and alluring, her constant cigarette smoking ravaged her body, left her with a persistent incurable cough and cast a lifeless sheen over her now leathery skin. Bonnie had changed in spirit as well. Clyde would think back to when he met her; the words he used to describe her on their wedding day were beautiful, sweet and joyful. With each passing year, Clyde replaced each of those with a new adjective — unpleasant, callous and mean. Whereas once she smelled like cotton candy outside on a spring day, her liver had started to turn and the harsh, yellow-scented perfume she used to cover up the overpowering aroma of old smoke forced a gagging sensation to swell up to the base of his throat every time Clyde sat next to her.

For a brief while, Clyde had also thought about dissolving the marriage. He even approached a few attorneys last year to discuss fees. But the cost of a long, drawn-out divorce would be catastrophic, considering his low salary, and in the end he could never let it happen. No matter what she'd become, Bonnie was his wife and no one else's. Clyde could never let another man have her fully and completely. But he couldn't live with her either. Late at night after his wife had erupted into a vodka-induced snore, Clyde would roll off the bed and sit on the floor, crying and wishing for a peaceful end. He had to kill her. If he didn't, he would kill himself.

So far Clyde had made three unsuccessful attempts at ending Bonnie's life.

Attempt One: At her cousin's bungalow, Clyde dropped a heavy cinderblock on Bonnie's head from the rooftop fifteen feet above. He'd spent weeks planning the specifics of the attack. Nothing was left to chance. The width and length of the block, the distance to the ground, the relative trajectory of the object. Wind resistance. Clyde had thought of it all. The attack would be as systematic as he was methodical in planning it. The only problem was that Clyde never expected the block to be so damn hard to move. It must have weighed 130 pounds and for the life of him Clyde couldn't imagine how Bonnie's cousin got it up on the roof in the first place. As Bonnie approached, he tested the wind with his finger and then tried to push the block off with his boot. It wouldn't budge. He started kicking it now. Bits of cinder dust scattered in the wind. Finally he knelt down on one knee just as he'd done for his bride years before and shoved the stone slab over the edge. Alas, the cinder block barely grazed her temple and Bonnie spent only three days in the hospital and required no more than a dozen trips to rehab.

Attempt Two: Following a rehab session, as Clyde assisted Bonnie in through the back door of their building, he pointed out a large ceramic unicorn sitting in the far corner of an open garbage Dumpster. Bonnie, who had an infatuation with tawdry velvet murals and ornate keepsakes, immediately got excited and vowed to return later that evening to fish it out of the debris. When she came back a few hours later, Bonnie climbed into the garbage bin only to discover someone had rigged a string around the unicorn's leg. The moment she pulled on the unicorn, the garbage bin lid slammed shut and trapped poor Bonnie inside. Clyde, the mastermind who planted the mythical creature in the bin, had intended to starve or suffocate Bonnie to death. Only his plan proved ill-conceived — there was not only a wide crack in which his wife could suck in air, but the Dumpster was used by a local restaurant, giving Bonnie piles of edible garbage on which she could feast for weeks on end. Much to Clyde's chagrin, less than an hour elapsed before a maintenance worker heard her screams and released her. The ceramic unicorn now stood as an umbrella holder in their front hall.

Attempt Three: Bonnie was severely allergic to peanuts. At dinner with Bonnie's parents one night, under the pretense of being silly, Clyde tossed a peanut into Bonnie's open mouth. His aim was true and good fortune was on his side as the felonious nut ricocheted off her tongue and bounced straight to the back of her throat, where it lodged squarely in her esophagus. She gasped and gagged as Clyde pretended to try to save her. It was all going incredibly well until an insolent young man ran out from the kitchen and pulled the peanut from Bonnie's throat using a pair of salad tongs.

Bonnie, for her part, had yet to notice Clyde was trying to murder her; she'd been too busy trying to kill him to notice. And this is how the two of them had lived for several months, with homicidal intent in their souls but without the cleverness or proficiency to pull off their respective crimes. During this time, neither of them gave any indication that something was wrong. They still kissed one another in the morning and chatted about their days when they returned home from work.

Twenty-four hours after the incident in the marketplace, Bonnie sat down to read her morning newspaper. She checked the lottery numbers and sighed a little when she saw that hers hadn't been picked. Bonnie's numbers were 1, 2, 3, 4, 5 and 6. She chose them based on the assumption that since six numbers are picked randomly, the sequence of 1, 2, 3, 4, 5, 6 was equally as possible as the numbers that won this time — 4, 15, 22, 33, 35, 48. Bonnie never realized that there were at least a thousand other jackasses across the country who routinely picked 1, 2, 3, 4, 5, 6 and made the same silly assertion. Were she ever to win, the four million dollar jackpot would be split a thousand ways, still winning her a sizable sum of money, but a patently demoralizing amount once she came down from the euphoria of thinking she'd hit the true jackpot.

Bonnie reached inside her purse and pulled out the lottery ticket she'd bought at the market to check it just in case. To her surprise, the numbers on her ticket weren't in sequence. The cashier had handed her the young man's ticket by mistake. A smile spread over Bonnie's face when the first number matched. Then the second number matched as well. Bonnie stared at the ticket in staggering astonishment. Her eyes shuffled back to the newspaper and then the ticket again. All six numbers were the same. This ticket — the one with the numbers the young man had picked — was the winner. Bonnie had just won four million dollars!

From the next room, a set of footsteps sounded. Quickly, Bonnie hid the ticket back in her purse. Her husband Clyde wandered into the kitchen and poured himself a cup of coffee.

"Good morning," she said.

Clyde looked at her out of the corner of his eye but didn't respond.

"Big day planned?" she said.

Clyde gave her that same look. "I told you the other day, I think I'm giving up caffeine," he said and poured his coffee into the sink without even taking a sip. It was a good thing. The cup was laced with arsenic.

Clyde noticed the expression on his wife's face.

"What's up?"

Bonnie could barely contain her excitement.

"Nothing," she said.

"Are you sure?"

"Of course."

Clyde threw his jacket over his shoulder and kissed his wife goodbye. Bonnie kissed him back. She even opened her mouth a little more than usual.

"I'll see you tonight."

"I'll miss you," she said.

Clyde left the apartment and Bonnie pulled out the ticket again. She checked the numbers one more time. The euphoria burned in her chest. With one final glance, she tucked the ticket back in her purse and thought about Clyde. There was no way she was going to share the money with him. Maybe if he respected her job a little more, if he'd shown the occasional burst of encouragement or congratulated her on her promotion, she might be inclined to give him half. But no. He was an irrefutable fiend and he had to die.

Bonnie would have to double her efforts.

five

Henrik Nordmark had spent the past twenty-four hours experiencing a rollercoaster ride of emotions. He set out to redefine himself — or rather to define himself in the first place. For hours on end, he tried everything he could think of and when he felt himself about to give up, he remembered Ronnie James Dio's prophetic words at a 1981 Black Sabbath concert (which Henrik had accidentally stumbled upon while in search of a flea market) — "If you want to be successful, you have to be unique." If Ronnie James Dio said it, it had to be true.

Henrik started by stripping off all his clothes and standing in front of a full-length mirror. He held his gratuitous pot belly in his hands and gave it a good shake. Perhaps, he decided, physical fitness could be his unique characteristic. Henrik had once seen a bodybuilding competition at a local fairground in which the gargantuan men on stage all had rippling, pulsating muscles. The men would flex their giant biceps and the crowd erupted in applause. They squeezed their *toight* buttocks and heard a chorus of lamentations from the women. Some of their muscles, like those triangle-shaped ones on their backs, Henrik wasn't even sure he had. Nevertheless, he was undaunted. The regular man could become physically fit. And it didn't even have to take that long. The Jamaican woman who worked the security night shift had recently lost thirty pounds on a program called Body For Life, which promised to give you the body you've always dreamed of in three months or less. Henrik even overheard her telling one of her friends how great she felt. He decided that he would feel great as well. Henrik fell to the floor, stark naked, and set about doing sit-ups. He accomplished three partial crunches before his back began to ache and he felt a dull pain in his abdomen. Henrik didn't understand. He was supposed to feel great. He most certainly did not.

After a strenuous attempt at a fourth sit-up, Henrik gave up on exercise. He decided there must be other ways to manipulate his appearance and make himself more noticeable. Henrik hastily put on his clothes and headed over to a nearby secondhand clothing store, where he purchased the most garish items he could find on the rack. Back home, he pulled on a pair of super-tight velvet bellbottom pants. Henrik laced them up underneath his belly and then wrapped a skull-printed headband around his forehead and pulled a fluorescent yellow, half cropped Menudo-era T-shirt over his chest. Henrik stood in front of the mirror. He looked like an insane person.

Perhaps some music will help, Henrik thought. He walked over to his cassette deck and pressed play. The only cassette he owned was the *Flashdance* soundtrack. A woman at a yard sale had thrown in the cassette as a sympathetic bonus when Henrik purchased her old, non-functioning Ikea lamp. Henrik pressed play and the first few synthesizer sounds of "What a Feeling" emitted from the stereo's fuzzy speakers. Henrik did interpretive dance moves to the slow portion before shaking his arms wildly and breaking out into full maniacal movement.

Henrik stopped himself before the song finished. He looked like an idiot. The point was to be unique and distinct, not downright ridiculous. He stripped off his clothes and tossed them in the trash and then flopped in front of the television.

His old black and white television received only three channels: the weather network, a religious station and NBC. On NBC tonight there was a *Dateline* special — *To Catch a Predator*. For an hour, Henrik watched as countless men were busted for soliciting sex from minors over the internet. He found this show to be infinitely fascinating. Each felon followed the same script. They would spend days, sometimes weeks, flirting with a teenage girl in an internet chat room before finally arranging a live, in-person meeting in which they were supposed to have sex. Only what they didn't know was that the teenage girl they were flirting with was actually a middle-aged police officer named Frank who had a moustache, a gut three times the size of Henrik's and, from the look of him, most likely some sort of foul stench emanating from his armpits. The predators would show up at a designated house expecting underage sex but instead they were accosted by Chris Hansen, a courageous reporter with a full head of excellent hair and rampant moral superiority. For some strange reason, when confronted by the handsome Chris Hansen, each and every one of the predators admitted exactly why they had come to the house, then once they found out they were going to be on national television, they cried, begged for forgiveness and left the house, appearing somewhat surprised when there were police officers standing outside to arrest them. To be fair, some of the predators didn't cry. But they all looked like they were about to cry and in Henrik's mind, that was as good as crying.

Henrik thought the idea of sex with a minor was completely repugnant. But he considered this all to be a matter of age and attraction, and wasn't quite sure what role moral accountability played in all of this. While he found sex with a minor to be an abominable act, he found sex with a senior citizen to be equally as abhorrent. However, if he were to be pressed into a decision — if, for example, some evil supervillain was holding the world hostage and valorous Henrik, as the last remaining member of a dying breed of superheroes, was forced to fornicate in order to save the planet from certain destruction with the one catch being that he had to choose either a minor or a senior to fornicate with, Henrik knew that deep in his heart of hearts, he would never — *never* — choose the senior. That Henrik could find such monstrosity within himself to be a child molester, albeit only in the due course of courageous service to mankind and only as a very last resort . . . the thought of it sent a flush of endorphins rushing to his brain where the opiate receptors responded in a pang of delight. He — Henrik Nordmark — might actually be depraved! Depravity had to be better than dullness. It just had to be.

Henrik clapped his hands in victory and suddenly fell sullen again. The clapping sound reminded him of a 1978 episode of *Super Friends* in which the Wonder Twins' sidekick Gleek was put in a trance and forced to commit all sorts of outrageous atrocities until he heard Robin the Boy Wonder clapping his hands and came to his senses, establishing that anyone can perform abominable acts under the right circumstances, given duress and good intentions in his heart. Henrik realized he wasn't super at all. He wasn't extraordinary. He would never be a superhero, or even a supervillain for that matter. At best he could aspire to the heights of comedic relief sidekick, and not even that — comedic relief monkey side-kick with limited speech capabilities.

Henrik turned off the television. He left his home and wandered the streets as the hour approached midnight. Two women passed him on their way to a local dance club, one of whom bore a striking resemblance to a young lady Henrik had stood beside in a grocery store lineup last week. Pink sunglasses, flowing blond hair, diamonds beaming from her fingers, neck and navel — that other woman had been holding a basket filled with cosmetic supplies and a four-pack of single-roll toilet paper. Henrik had waddled up next to her carrying a Costco-sized pack of forty-eight industrial-strength double-ply extra-fortified toilet rolls. The pretty young girl in line glanced at Henrik out of the corner of her eye. The glance lasted for the briefest of moments, a miniscule blip on the timeline of human history, but long enough to convey to Henrik the omnipresent, relentless truth — that this woman thought he was a monster who does nothing but sit on a porcelain bowl, magazine in hand, and poop all day and night long.

This woman and her friend were dressed to the nines with wild hair, sultry makeup and plentiful exposed cleavage. Henrik imagined what it would be like to kiss one or maybe even both of these women — how their wet tongues would taste like cherries and pink marshmallows. He leered brazenly at their breasts and felt himself ridiculous for doing so. Henrik pictured a painful, demoralizing scene in a discotheque in which he would approach these fine young women and ask them to dance . . . only to be ridiculed, or worse — ignored. *Yes*, Henrik decided, *that is exactly what these women would do. They would ignore me. So I will ignore them.* Henrik turned his eyes away from their supple bosoms. For a second or two as they passed, Henrik felt morally superior. Their exposed cleavage would not control him. He was no Pavlovian dog.

In the end, Henrik's moral outrage was all for naught. The women didn't even notice him staring the other way. They were too busy texting on their cell phones to even look up.

He passed an all-night internet café when suddenly inspiration struck. Henrik was only boring to the rest of the world because they could see him. They could sense from his outward physical appearance, from the way he carried himself and from the smell of discount laundry detergent in his clothes that he wasn't worthy of their interest. But in the virtual world there were no such concerns. Virtual communication was purely intellectual. Perhaps in this abstract realm, Henrik could shine in the way he'd always dreamt of shining. Henrik entered the café, paid for an hour's worth of internet time and then sat down at the nearest computer. He stared at the open Internet Explorer window in front of him. The default Google page had a text box with a slow, repetitively flashing cursor. At first, Henrik didn't know what to type. So he entered the words "chat room" and 54,900,000 sites returned. Undaunted, Henrik began scrolling through them. After nearly entering a chat room dedicated to the drastic alterations North Korea had made to Anne Frank's diary, he stumbled across a room where people met online to discuss the singer and poet Jewel. Henrik had actually heard one of her songs on the radio. It was pretty good. She wasn't quite the wordsmith Ronnie James Dio had been in his prime — but then again, who was?

Henrik entered the chat room, signed in with his real

name and typed the words "I am obsessed with Jewel." There were only two other members currently chatting. Neither of them acknowledged Henrik. He tried again.

Henrik Nordmark – I am obsessed with Jewel
Sassycat8 – Did you see her on David Letterman last week?
Atc_Xtreme – yes, I did. She looked beautiful, snaggle tooth and all
Sassycat8 – have you ever seen her live in concert?
Henrik Nordmark – I saw Black Sabbath play a concert in 1981
Atc_Xtreme – really? Ozzy Osbourne rocks !!!!!
Henrik Nordmark – who's Ozzy Osbourne?
Atc_Xtreme – he's the singer for Black Sabbath
Henrik Nordmark – No, Ronnie James Dio is the singer for Black Sabbath
Atc_Xtreme – no, he's not
Henrik Nordmark – yes, he is
Sassycat8 – doesn't anyone want to talk about Jewel?
[Saintdameon has entered the room]
Saintdameon – my balls really itch when I fuck fat chicks
Atc_Xtreme – that's just gross
[Atc_Xtreme has left the room]
Sassycat8 – I'm leaving. This chat room sucks . . .
[Sassycat8 has left the room]
Henrik Nordmark –
Henrik Nordmark –
Saintdameon – so Henrik, what do you have to say for yourself?
Henrik Nordmark –
Henrik Nordmark –
Henrik Nordmark –
Saintdameon – nothing?
Henrik Nordmark – I am obsessed with Jewel
[Saintdameon has left the room]

Henrik departed the internet café even more upset than when he entered. His boring conversation had made people flee his presence. Were there any depths lower than the one to which he'd just sunk? Henrik headed straight home and turned on the television again. He watched a cooking show with Rachael Ray, considered masturbating to her segment about making goulash, then heard her thick New York accent and suddenly fell limp. He changed the channel to Jacksonville's Religious Crusade. Henrik watched this show with eager fascination. One after another guests came on to explain what an incredible impact Jesus had made in their lives. The outdated hairstyles and grainy film quality made Henrik suspect he was watching a rerun. But there was a 1-800 number at the bottom of the screen. Henrik was willing to try anything — even giving up his life of brazen heresy. He'd never considered becoming a religious zealot before. It did seem to have its advantages. The sense of righteous indignation and the promise of an eternal life were both alluring. Henrik couldn't really think of a third reason, but he repeated the first two in his head and decided they more than justified his looking into this.

He picked up the phone and called the number.

A woman with a southern accent answered.

"Hello, this is Mary Jo. Would you like to donate to Jacksonville's Religious Crusade?"

"Actually," Henrik said, "I'd just like to learn more about your religion."

"Would you like to subscribe to the Jacksonville's Religious Crusade newsletter?"

"Yes, I would."

Unprompted, Henrik gave the woman all his personal

details — address, birthdate, social insurance number, bank account number and his PIN numbers.

"Sir, I don't think we need all of that information."

"Is there someone I can talk to about Jesus now?" Henrik said.

"You would have to call a different number for that," the woman said. "I work primarily in the donations department."

There was something funny about this woman. Her accent was inconsistent. It wavered from Deep Southern, to Southern Baptist, to something altogether foreign. Norwegian, maybe?

"So there's no one there that I can talk to about religion?" Henrik said.

"I'm afraid not, sir. You would have to call a different number."

"Do you have that number?" he said.

"No, I don't. Not in front of me."

"Oh."

There was dead silence on the line. Finally, the woman spoke. Her southern accent suddenly disappeared and was replaced by another accent altogether.

"Listen, sir, I have to level with you," she said. "My name isn't Mary Jo. It's Parminder. The Jacksonville Religious Crusade outsourced their financial calls to India three weeks ago. People were getting really angry when they heard my Indian accent, so I started faking an American accent. I'm sorry to have misled you."

"Outsourced?" Henrik said.

"Yes, you know how things are with the global economy and whatnot."

"And you answer all of Jacksonville's Religious Crusade's calls?"

"I sometimes also pick up calls for the Ab Lounger Deluxe."

"Does that machine really work?" Henrik said.

"No," she said. "I don't think it does."

"How much do they pay you?"

"One hundred and forty-five rupees an hour."

"How much is that?" he said.

"I believe it's about three dollars and fifty cents."

"Really?"

"Yes, really," she said.

"And you can't teach me about Jesus?"

"No," she said. "I'm not Christian. I'm Sikh. I follow the teachings of Nanak."

"I want to learn about religion so that I can be different," Henrik said. "I want to be unique."

"Well, religion alone won't make you unique." Parminder suddenly turned somewhat philosophical. "That's something you need to find within yourself."

"What if it's not there?" Henrik said. "What if there isn't anything within me to make me unique?"

Parminder didn't seem to know what to say so she began explaining Nanak and the writings of the Janamsakhis. Apparently Nanak believed in helping the elderly and the poor. This was all very well and good, Henrik thought, as it is probably the wisest way to attract virtuous people to one's religion. Henrik leaned back in his chair and listened intently for almost three full minutes before feeling abnormally tired. Parminder's real accent was quite thick and difficult to understand. Moreover, this Nanak seemed to speak in a lot of generalities. Henrik wondered if Jesus spoke in so many generalities. His eyelids were getting heavy. A wave of drowsiness washed over him.

Henrik was just about to fall asleep when he heard a second voice on the line. A man with an even thicker Indian accent was speaking to Parminder in a language Henrik didn't recognize. Parminder replied in the same language. They carried on for about fifteen seconds before the man's voice trailed off into the distance.

"I'm sorry," Parminder said. "My supervisor walked by and asked me what I was talking about."

"Did I get you in trouble?" Henrik said.

"Nothing I can't handle," Parminder said. "I do have to go though. Donations to the Crusade are down eight percent this quarter and I have an hourly rate to maintain. But I wish you the best, Henrik. Be strong my friend. And have faith that you will find what you're looking for."

She hung up.

Henrik turned off the television and placed his phone on the receiver. He waddled on groggy feet into the bedroom and climbed under the covers. Henrik put his head on the pillow, completely unaware that at that very moment on the other side of town, three elderly assassins were planning his demise.

six

9:37 a.m. Alfred's 1984 Chrysler LeBaron thundered along the road with pockets of rust on the hood and billows of black smoke churning out the back. Like an out-of-control shopping cart, it warbled down a hill, veered between lanes and narrowly missed a stop sign as Alfred's shaky hands steered the vehicle off the highway and into the suburbs. Beside Alfred, dressed in black from head to toe, Conrad barked out sightless directions to his mute associate and held on for dear life.

Billy Bones sat in the back seat, a smile spread across his frumpy face.

The previous evening in the dead of night, Alfred and Billy Bones sneaked out of their rooms and met Conrad in a darkened corner of the retirement home. There amongst the shadows, Conrad laid out plans for their mission. Billy Bones, fearing it might be his last, insisted he be allowed to say goodbye to his one true love. Conrad and Alfred naturally assumed he meant his wife of fifty-three years, a woman named Beatrice who lived in a nursing home across town. When they mentioned her name, Billy Bones went red with anger.

"Beatrice tried to kill me with a meat cleaver back in 1976. Why would I want to see her?"

"Really, old chap?" Conrad said. "You've never told me this before."

"I came home from the track smelling like perfume, and

Beatrice, who was an old biddy years before she was old enough to be an old biddy, she grabbed a meat cleaver and swung it at my head. I ducked out of the way and she hit our cat Mittens."

"Dear God."

"Split the cat right in two, she did. It made a hell of a sound."

"What happened after she killed the cat?"

"That's where the story gets ugly. Beatrice didn't quite manage to kill the cat. Mittens proved resilient. Cats with orange hair have always got a lot of fight in them. She rushed Mittens to the vet and he sewed him up pretty good. Somehow Mittens managed to hang on for the better part of six months. He would hobble around the house howling in pain. Beatrice always blamed me. She told me the cat developed low self-esteem since it wasn't able to catch mice anymore. But I told her — *you* swung the meat cleaver!"

"And now you're estranged?" Conrad said.

"We are."

"Then who is this true love of yours?"

Billy Bones motioned for Conrad to come closer. Of course, the room was dark and Conrad was blind so he couldn't see. He stood still, waiting expectantly. Billy Bones leaned into Conrad's ear and screamed, "A prostitute I visited during the war! Rosalina Estranova!"

Conrad recoiled from Billy's bellowing voice. His hands formed a pyramid under his chin and his expression turned serious. "I will find this Rosalina Estranova for you, old friend. You will say your goodbyes and then we'll settle the business at hand."

The next day Conrad made a few calls and it turned out

there was a woman named Rosalina Estranova living about twenty minutes from the old folks' home. They climbed into Alfred's car and despite not having had a valid driver's license for the past fifteen years and the fact his insurance had long since expired, Alfred fired up the old LeBaron and roared off. Soon enough they rounded the last corner before the Estranova household.

Conrad stepped out of the car and into the backdrop of a green suburban landscape, his crimson-laced cape fluttering in the breeze. On the road, children were playing street hockey. Alfred had narrowly missed running into a goal-tender and a defenseman as he parked the car. He peered his long pointed nose through the open window and climbed out on thin legs to stand beside Conrad. Billy Bones waited behind as the two old assassins approached the house. The front door was painted Amsterdam red.

"Now remember," Conrad said. "Old Bones wants us to scope out the situation first to make sure this is a good idea."

Alfred nodded. He dusted off his old brown suit, secured his pocket watch inside his vest, then rang the doorbell.

A count of ten passed before the door opened to reveal a stunning young Spanish woman, her skin luminous and brown. The long curls of her black hair fell down to her shoulders where they met the transparent white of her dress. The dress, in turn, clung to her skin, curved tight along her waist and led to the plunging neckline that displayed her pert breasts. She was a goddess. A warmth swirled in Alfred's heart. Beside him, the ethereal smell from the woman's sun-browned skin caused Conrad's ancient loins to ache. She couldn't have been more than twenty-three years old.

"We're looking for Rosalina Estranova."

"You've found her," the young woman said.

Alfred leaned over and whispered something inaudible in Conrad's ear. Conrad pushed him away. "I believe we're looking for someone more senior."

The young woman shifted her weight from one sumptuous hip to the other.

"You're thinking of my grandmother. Grandma Rosa died late last year. I'm looking after her house while the estate is being contested."

Conrad twirled the ends of his moustache. "This might be a slightly delicate question, my dear, but was your grandmother a prostitute during the war?"

The young woman opened her mouth to speak and then paused. Her moist bottom lip kept Alfred mesmerized.

"Have you by any chance taken up the family business?" Conrad said.

"I'm an exotic dancer," she said. "Not a prostitute."

"Then the apple hasn't fallen all that far from the tree."

"Rosalina!" Billy called from the car. "You're as beautiful as the day I last saw you." He stepped out and began shuffling up the front walk.

Conrad leaned into the young woman's ear. "Time is of the essence and I can't explain in full, but I will give you five hundred dollars if you pretend to be your grandmother for fifteen minutes."

The young woman shifted her eyes from Conrad to Billy Bones and back to Conrad again.

"A thousand," she said.

Conrad reached out his glove and handed her a wad of crisp one-hundred-dollar bills. Rosalina took the money just as Billy Bones enveloped her in a full-body hug.

"What's his name?" she said.

"Bones. And there's no need to whisper," Conrad said. "My associate is quite deaf."

Billy Bones stepped back to give her a better look. "My goodness," he said. "You haven't aged a day."

"Would you like to come in for some tea?" the young woman said at the top of her voice.

Billy Bones shook Alfred's hand. He clasped Conrad's glove as well. "I'll be back in ten minutes, boys. Light a candle for me."

With that Billy Bones and his true love's granddaughter disappeared through the front door. Conrad and Alfred took position by the LeBaron and waited. They soon discovered they had an audience. The children playing street hockey had stopped their game and watched the whole scene take place. A couple of parents had now appeared and were casting suspicious looks at the two elderly assassins who were now leaning against the car. The tall skinny one smoked cigarettes while staring back at them in silence as the one in the cape slapped a pair of gloves against his shiny black cane.

Twenty minutes later the red door opened and Billy Bones emerged. Alfred could have sworn he saw the young Rosalina Estranova behind him, adjusting her dress back into its rightful position.

"Onward and upward," Billy Bones yelled. "We have a mission to accomplish."

The three associates climbed into the old boat. A burst of black smog shot out the back as Alfred put the car in gear and tore backward out of the driveway. The goaltender and defenseman leapt out of the way as Alfred knocked over a flimsy hockey net before peeling off down the street.

 seven

Henrik marched toward the employment office, quite determined for such an early hour in the day. He stopped outside the building and gazed up at the big blue letters emblazoned above the doors. *Employment Office.* The words themselves were daunting. Henrik had narrowed his quest for distinction to one of two options when he awoke that morning: Try to find a new job or try to find a girlfriend. The mere thought of the latter stirred in Henrik's chest such a fretful swell that he thought he might burst a blood vessel and had to sit down for a couple of minutes to calm down.

He resolved instead to find an exciting profession, the type of job that by definition would make him unique.

In twenty years, Henrik had never considered leaving his security guard post. There were so many benefits to his current work. True, he was required to stand most of the day and it was demoralizing to have so many people pass by as though he were a wooden statue in a cigar store window. But the job was straightforward with few demands for physical exertion and he wasn't required to produce quantifiable results in order to keep his employer happy. Henrik also found he was rarely called upon to quell disturbances.

When he first took the post as a young man, Henrik anticipated the day might arrive when he would be called upon to act courageously — to throw his body in the way of a bullet or fend off a trespasser with his billy club. In truth, he never planned on jumping in front of a gun or taking out his nightstick. But from the moment he put on the uniform, he anticipated that others would respect him as someone who might act with valor in the course of duty.

Nothing could have been further from the truth. Henrik was routinely ignored. From the attractive women in their business suits, the most he could hope for was a dismissive head nod, and even that seemed to be a colossal chore requiring such superhuman effort that he couldn't hope for more than three head nods a week. Henrik's duties were so mundane that within an hour of working his post that very first day, he found himself sleepwalking through his job, much in the way he'd sleepwalked through life.

"Not anymore," he said.

Henrik entered the employment office. The place was teeming with people, men and women, young and old, some with children, others wedged two to a seat in the small green chairs, all waiting for their names to be called. The room had the air of a refugee camp in which people hunker down for days at a time because they have nowhere else to go. Henrik almost expected a live chicken to pop out of someone's handbag and run frantically around the floor as famished, unemployed jobseekers chased after it. He walked up to the front desk where a lady was reading the newspaper.

"I would like to find a new job," he said.

She snapped her bubblegum. "Please take a number, sir. You'll have to wait three hours before we issue you an employment insurance check."

"But I don't want a check. I want to find a job that makes me unique."

A tiny sparkle formed in the corner of the lady's eye.

"Wow, we don't usually get one of you in here," she said. She stood up and rummaged excitedly through a stack of papers on her desk. The lady found the page she was looking for, attached it to a clipboard and handed it to Henrik. "Please fill this out." She glanced around the room. "You might have trouble finding a seat."

"I'll sit on the bench out front," he said.

"Excellent. I'll call you soon."

Henrik sat in front of the employment office and dutifully filled out the entire sheet. He listed his name and age, the number of years he'd been working in his current occupation, and in the box next to the question, "What is your dream job?" Henrik wrote "florist" — the first profession he could think of that was equal parts innocuous and difficult to mock. He turned the page over to find a list of occupations with instructions to circle those that interested him the most.

Henrik had circled a few when an incident broke out in the lot next door. Two men were having a disagreement over a parking space. As the argument raged on, it became clear the driver of a red Honda Civic had parked in a spot that was actually a walkway. The other man was the building manager, livid that people kept parking in this non-regulation spot.

"Listen," the car owner said. "I'll just move my vehicle and get out of your way."

The building manager stepped in front of the driver's side door. "We've called the tow truck company and we're towing this vehicle."

"There's not even a tow truck in sight," the car owner

said. "You can't honestly expect me to wait around until the tow truck shows up."

"That's exactly what I expect you to do. You parked in a walkway and now people can't get through."

The car owner, a man wearing a Dunkin' Donuts uniform, ran his hands through his hair in frustration. "What's more important?" he said. "Moving this car so people can walk by or punishing me for parking here?"

Faced with the irrefutable logic of this argument, the stubborn building manager crossed his arms and stood in front of the driver's side door.

Quickly, in a sudden unexpected move, the car owner scurried around the vehicle and jammed his keys into the lock on the passenger side. As he turned the key, the building manager grabbed him and a small skirmish broke out in which the two men struggled against the car door. In the end, the Dunkin' Donuts employee escaped into the confines of his car and managed to lock the door before driving away. The only damage done was a budding bruise on the building manager's jaw and a long, angular scrape across the Honda Civic's car bra.

Henrik watched the incident take place with surreal wonder, as though it were a scene from a movie and not real life. During the skirmish, he wondered whether there wasn't some sort of implicit societal obligation for him to enter the fray and defuse the situation. And if he was thus duty-bound, and the situation were to get completely out of hand, which side would he choose?

The lady from the employment office opened the door and took the clipboard from Henrik. "Mr. Nordmark, one of our employment specialists will see you now."

Henrik was ushered into a tiny office at the end of a long corridor. He glanced around the room. The bookshelves contained no books at all but rather stacks of multi-colored file folders lined up next to boxes wrapped in brown paper. Henrik sat down in front of an empty desk and was joined shortly by a man wearing a brown suit and a green tie. The man took his seat at the desk and immediately started doing paperwork. Henrik looked him up and down. His eyes darted around the cluttered office and then focused straight on the man's tie.

The man put his paperwork aside. "Now, how can I help you today?"

"I want to find a job that makes me unique."

"What's your previous occupation?"

"Security guard," Henrik said.

"Well that's not very unique at all. There are thousands of security guards out there."

"That's my point exactly. I need a job that, by definition, makes me unique."

The man in the green tie picked up the clipboard with the list of occupations. He scanned the sheet for the ones Henrik circled. "Let me see here. Aerospace Engineer, Professional Bodybuilder, Lactation Consultant. Do you have any expertise in these areas? Any aerospace training?"

"No, sir. I don't."

"Any weightlifting or bodybuilding skills?"

Henrik covered his pot belly with his arms. "No."

"What about this last one — Lactation Consultant? Do you have a specific proficiency in this area?"

"Actually," Henrik said, "I wasn't a hundred percent sure what that one was."

"It's when you help new mothers learn to breastfeed their babies."

Henrik grimaced. "No. I don't care how unique it makes me. I don't want to do that."

The man in the green tie leaned forward in his chair. He glanced from side to side and then looked Henrik straight in the eye. "Mr. Nordmark, do you know how you really make money in this world?"

"How?"

"You get other people to work for you."

"Do you mean by hiring employees and providing some kind of goods or service? Because that seems like a great deal of work."

The man in the green tie walked around to Henrik's side of the desk. He dragged an old dust-covered ottoman toward the center of the room and sat down with one leg over the other.

"The trick, you see, is that you don't need to provide any goods or services. You don't need an office and you don't need to pay any of your employees."

Henrik's ears perked.

"What you need to do is find entrepreneurs. Well, not full-fledged entrepreneurs, but people with an entrepreneurial spirit who lack direction. And you give them direction. You help them to go out and realize their capitalist dreams while you sit back with your feet up, drinking piña coladas and lounging by the pool all day, all the while collecting ten percent of their earnings just for helping them get started."

"But wouldn't these entrepreneurs want to do the same thing?" Henrik said. "Wouldn't they want to find people to work for them so that they could put their feet up and drink expensive cocktails?"

"That's the beauty of the whole plan. The entrepreneurs you find will go out and find ten more people and then those people will find ten people and so on."

"But at the end of the day, wouldn't someone have to do some kind of work to bring in money?"

"Of course. But it won't be you."

Henrik furrowed his brow. "You're talking about a pyramid scheme. I don't want to be involved in a pyramid structure of any kind."

"That's not true," the man in the green tie said. "You don't want to be at the bottom of the pyramid. But I bet you'd love to be at the top. Everybody wants to be at the top of a pyramid made of money."

"I really don't think it's for me."

Henrik started to leave. The man in the green tie placed his hand on Henrik's shoulder. "Mr. Nordmark, you don't really want to be a florist, do you?"

"No, I don't."

"Now, I wasn't going to tell you about this because I've been keeping it a secret. But I like you. You seem like a trustworthy person. My idea is for a new type of service which up until this point has never been attempted before. This is still in the conceptual stage," the man said, "but my business will be called the Truth Company."

"What will you sell?" Henrik said.

"We'll sell the truth."

"But isn't the truth free?"

"No, it isn't," the man's hands grew animated as he spoke. "Most companies routinely lie. They lie to stockholders. They lie to consumers and employees. They deceive and swindle and finagle as a daily part of their operations. The

Truth Company will be different, Mr. Nordmark. We'll sell the truth.

"Say for instance you work in an office where you're generally happy. The people are nice and the work is inane, but bearable. Everything is fine except for one thing that drives you crazy. For example, one of your coworkers chats constantly on the phone about her upcoming wedding. Or another coworker might have really offensive body odor. What do you do about this? How do you tell them the truth?"

"It would be socially awkward to say something."

"Yes! Exactly," the man's voice swelled. "That's why the Truth Company will do it for you. You pay the Truth Company to tell the person that nobody cares that all the good places are booked or what color their centerpieces will be. To tell them to take a bath and wear deodorant, for Christ's sake. Now this can happen in several ways. For a nominal cost, the Truth Company will send an anonymous note to the person explaining their offense in detail and listing the negative consequences their insensitivity has incurred on those around them. For an additional cost, in the case of body odor — which incidentally, I suspect will be the company's top moneymaker — we'll include a bar of soap and a stick of deodorant. Now, I'm just thinking off the top of my head here, but perhaps a secondary stream of revenue can come from cross-promotion with one of the national deodorant stick companies."

Henrik was intrigued, although he was not ready to subscribe to this man's newsletter just yet. "Go on."

"In the case a client believes an anonymous note won't send a strong enough message, for an additional fee the Truth Company will send out a field operative to confront the offender and tell them what they've done straight to their face." The man in the brown suit and green tie leaned back on the ottoman. "In fact, I'm looking for field operatives right now. You have an opportunity here, Mr. Nordmark, to get in at the ground floor. Now, I can't pay you at first. But I'm a generous man. When the Truth Company grows into a worldwide entity, I won't soon forgot those who where loyal to me at the start. So, would this be something you might be interested in?"

"You want me to approach strangers and tell them they emit a foul stench from their armpits?"

"Your duties will be far more wide-ranging," he said. "But yes, that would be part of your job."

"What if someone punched me in the face?"

The man paused a beat.

"Then I'll buy you a Coke."

Henrik stood to leave.

"I tell you what." The man handed Henrik a handwritten pamphlet. "Read through this literature and let me know what you think. The clock is ticking, Mr. Nordmark. The time for opportunity is now."

Henrik thought it over. Perhaps there was something to what this man was saying. The world was full of lies and lying liars who perpetrate these falsehoods. Friends lie and strangers lie. Husbands lie to wives about where they've been all night and wives lie to husbands about why the milkman was in the house for an hour and a half. Parents are the worst perpetrators of all, what with their fictionalized deities like the Easter Bunny and the Tooth Fairy. There is nothing more unique than a beacon of truth in a world of perjury and fabrication. Yet what this man proposed seemed risky. First, there was no security of a weekly paycheck in order to afford the rent. And second, Henrik might get punched in the face.

No. He couldn't commit to this right now. Henrik shook the man's hand and left the employment office. He had to start work in less than two hours. Henrik ambled down the street, headed for a bookstore, completely unaware that in less than an hour's time, he would take his first steps along the journey to becoming utterly unique.

 eight

Roland sat down on the bench outside his office building. He reached inside his *Battle of the Planets* lunch box and pulled out a peanut butter sandwich, a mixed-berry juice box, two cheese sticks and a bag of Doritos. Roland steadfastly refused to eat in the cafeteria where lately the talk had been all about shifting corporate paradigms and Regis Philbin's ties. Instead, for the past two months when lunchtime came around he would sit on this bench and wait for the girls from the marketing department to walk by. Two of the six women were actually pretty cute and one of them usually wore a tight skirt. Some days Mason would join him but on this morning Roland's officemate was conspicuously absent from his cubicle. Roland could only imagine Mason had received the promotion. He set about reading yesterday's newspaper and waiting for the marketing girls to walk by.

As Roland opened his bag of chips, he flipped to the second page to check the winning lottery numbers. His heart lurched up into his throat and for a moment the world stopped moving. The winning numbers — 4, 15, 22, 33, 35, 48 — were the same numbers he'd played every week for years. Roland had just won four million dollars! He screamed out loud. Random passersby on the street gave him a curious look but Roland didn't care. He screamed again. The cute marketing girls exiting the main doors also gave him a funny look, but Roland couldn't stop screaming.

In a fit of euphoria, he searched his wallet for the ticket. A moment of panic almost overtook him when he couldn't immediately find it. Then Roland remembered he'd tucked the ticket into the back pocket of his jeans the other day. He ran straight home.

Roland's apartment was located on the ninth floor in the building directly above the marketplace where he'd purchased the ticket. He entered his bedroom and headed straight for the closet where he pulled out the pair of jeans. Delicately, with the tips of his fingers, he tugged on the piece of paper in the back right pocket. A quarter inch of paper jutted out. There it was: the blue and yellow lotto emblem at the top of the ticket. He pushed it back in and rolled his jeans into a ball. As fast as his legs could carry him, Roland ran to the bank where he placed the jeans in a safety deposit box. He never even bothered to pull out his ticket and take a look. Somewhere deep down, an irrational fear sprouted that were he to remove it from the pocket of his jeans, he might somehow lose it down a drainpipe or the oil from his skin might cause the numbers to run, thereby invalidating the ticket and stripping him of his winnings. Roland glanced at his watch. There was no reason to return to work today. He left the ticket and the jeans in the safety deposit box and planned to return for them tomorrow.

Roland headed off joyfully down the street, already planning the details of his new life. Things were going to change. Big things were going to happen for him.

But first, all of those corporate bastards at his work would have to pay.

 nine

Bonnie's plan came to her as a sudden revelation, a bolt of lightning that finally struck after years of rumbling thunder. A week ago a sign posted in the lobby of her building informed the residents that the elevator would be out of order for two full days. Bonnie immediately pictured Clyde — that bastard, that fiend — running in a full sprint toward the open elevator doors only to find a bottomless pit in its place. Clyde would careen down the elevator shaft while Bonnie stood safe and victorious at the top, dragging on a cigarette with cinematic light silhouetting her golden hair.

Right before Clyde finally landed fourteen floors down, she would utter a clever, poignant line, perhaps a little more clever than poignant; the kind of line film stars say in the second-to-last scene of an action movie the moment after they've vanquished their evil arch-nemesis who speaks with a foreign accent. Bonnie had considered several lines. Most of them were quite juvenile and contained phrases such as "die, you bastard" and "see you in hell." Still others were variations on famous movie lines: "hasta la vista, asshole" immediately came to mind.

Last night at work, it finally came to her. "You've been shafted." Clyde would have just long enough to hear her well timed quip and appreciate both how clever it was and how he'd gotten his just desserts before he made a horrible splat at the bottom of the empty elevator shaft.

Using euphemisms and a thinly veiled analogy, Bonnie explained the scenario to one of her coworkers as if it was a scene from a movie she'd seen on cable. "Get it?" she said. "He's been shafted, as in he fell down an elevator shaft."

Her friend didn't seem convinced.

"But the bad guy in the movie — he's a real jerk, right?"

"Of course he is."

"Well, if he deserves what's coming to him then he's not really getting shafted. He's just getting what he deserves."

Bonnie scratched her head. Her friend clearly didn't understand quite how cinematic this would all be. Perhaps she needed to be more sinister and vicious. Instead of Clyde accidentally happening upon the open elevator doors, Bonnie could bully her husband around, drag him by his hair and hurl him into the vacuous pit, the whole while emitting nothing but a primal scream. No, Bonnie said to herself. Her plan was solid. It was sound. She ignored the unhelpful advice and resolved not to tell anyone of her plans until they were carried through.

On the day the elevator was scheduled to be repaired, Bonnie could barely contain her excitement. She kissed Clyde goodbye as he left for work with a big smile on her face and extravagant plans to spend her lottery winnings in the back of her head. The sky was the limit. At last Bonnie could afford to purchase her dream car, a red 1969 Camaro convertible with lightning bolts painted down the sides. On a whim, she could log on to eBay and bid on all of the rare imported Hall & Oates albums money could buy. Most important of all, she could finally pay for the removal of the tattoo she'd received after a KISS concert twelve years ago when Gene Simmons — standing outside of a tour bus and wearing a baseball cap and cowboy boots — signed her left breast with a Sharpie. Less than an hour later the tattoo artist's ink was dry. Bonne's regret lasted much longer.

Her mind was swirling with all of the possibilities when Clyde gave her a hug and walked out the door for work. He had no idea his demise was less than ten hours away.

One can only imagine Bonnie's horror when she awoke from her afternoon nap to find the elevator fixed and running as normal. The maintenance crew had come by as she slept and resolved a minor mechanical issue. There would be no open elevator doors, no well timed one-liner slipping from her lips, no vacuous pit in which to throw Clyde.

Bonnie almost burst into tears. She flopped defeated on the couch and watched an old Foghorn Leghorn cartoon until Clyde came home.

"Do you want to go for a walk?" he said.

Bonnie dreaded the idea. She groaned and said, "To where?"

"We can walk over the Fraser Bridge."

Bonnie's ears perked up. The bridge rested two hundred feet above the Fraser River. Next to three lanes of traffic there existed only a narrow walkway on top and anyone who traversed it dangled precariously over the two-hundred-foot drop. Perhaps tonight wouldn't be a total loss after all.

Bonnie leapt off the couch and rooted around in the closet.

"Your jacket's on the chair," Clyde said.

"I'm looking for my hat," Bonnie said. She found her wool hat but continued rummaging in the back of the closet until she located Clyde's fishing kit. Bonnie removed a thick wooden stick with "The Clubber" emblazoned on its side and hid it inside her jacket before following Clyde out the door.

The married couple chatted as they walked toward the bridge. Clyde hated his job. Bonnie loved hers. Clyde was worried about money. Bonnie pretended she was too. In truth, the ecstatic glow never left her face. Clyde seemed to sense something was up. In the past twenty-four hours, he'd asked her six times if she had anything to tell him.

"You know, your father never understood you," she said.

"Thank you," Clyde said emphatically.

Bonnie smiled. It never failed. Any time she wanted to change the subject, particularly during an argument, all she had to do was mention Clyde's father. Clyde would immediately forget what they were fighting about and start listing every unfortunate incident from his childhood. Clyde's father — who looked like Clyde in every way, from his small nose and flaky brown haircut down to his long arms and slight shoulders — was a master beekeeper and like any master in his trade, wanted nothing more than for his son to follow in his footsteps. Clyde however, had neither an aptitude for the tiny creatures nor the desire to spend his adult life at constant risk of being swarmed. The science of it was all too much for him. His father would launch into a rage anytime Clyde was unable to remember the minute intricacies involving the invention of the Movable Comb Hive. Nor could young Clyde keep track of Colony Collapse Disorder and what it meant for a hive to be without a queen.

"He insisted I get stung once a day, every day so I would get used to it. Imagine the welts on my arms. Just think of the swelling. If only my father had listened to me, if only he understood me more as a person, I might have become something. Worst of all, he never encouraged my music."

"Music?" Bonnie said. This was a new one.

"I played the clarinet in eighth grade. And I was pretty good at it, my teacher even said so. But my father didn't care. While I was practicing, he would storm into the house wearing his white beekeeping outfit and his mesh mask, stray bees trailing him in the air, and demand that I stop my infernal racket because the queen bee didn't like my music. He threw my clarinet in the trash can behind the beehives. Then he forced me to get stung again."

"That's horrible!"

"I know," he said.

As they approached the bridge, Bonnie kept her hands in her pockets, the right one gripped tightly around The Clubber while Clyde ambled along beside her, alternately muttering about his father and humming the tune to an old heavy metal song he'd heard in high school. In the song, the boyfriend hurls his girlfriend off a bridge because he thinks she might break up with him. Clyde had no illusions that Bonnie would break up with him. Despite how callous and mean she'd gotten over the years, she seemed quite committed to the relationship. He looked over now at those gorgeous eyes that had once made his legs weak with puppy love. The rest of her might have changed, but the eyes, bright green and wide, were still the same.

Clyde almost felt bad that she had only minutes to live.

As they ascended the bridge deck, the last vestiges of sunlight streamed across the horizon, the light cut by ripples in the water. The sky changed from orange to purple and the clouds formed a tattered blanket through which the sun struggled desperately to shine. Bonnie took her hand out of her jacket and Clyde reached over and held it. Together they walked hand in hand toward the center of the bridge. The cars passing in the middle lanes were few and far between. They found themselves alone, husband and wife, holding hands and watching the sunset.

The purple light eventually faded, its hazy aura morphing into a delicate amethyst as night overtook the day. Clyde let go of Bonnie's hand and looked down at the water below. As black as night, the thick river water surged a little. Clyde started counting down in his head.

Ten.

Nine.

Eight.

Beside him Bonnie's free hand found the thick wooden club. She gripped it tight and looked up into the sky where the marbled clouds had dispersed to reveal an ocean of stars. She was momentarily overwhelmed by the enormity of it all.

Seven.

Six.

Five.

Bonnie took the stars in fully. She thought of her lottery winnings and how she would soon be standing next to a giant check with four million dollars and her name on it. Bonnie's imagination got the best of her and she started picturing the minutiae of the presentation. How the photographer would remind her to look into the camera. The solid handshake of the man from the lottery office. The emotional gambit she would run between jubilation and glee. Looking into the fading sky, what she was about to do seemed all wrong. True, Clyde was a ruthless cad, a wolf in sheep's clothing, a deceitful bastard if ever there was one. And he deserved to die. Of this Bonnie was certain.

But it was such a perfect evening.

Bonnie let go of the club and put her hand on Clyde's cheek. She brought him close and kissed him on the lips.

Clyde returned Bonnie's kiss but didn't stop counting.

Four.

Three.

Two.

"Hold me tight," Bonnie said and cuddled into her husband's coat. Clyde felt her chest press against his. Bonnie tucked her head under his chin and breathed in a long, comforting breath. Clyde knew he should ignore her. He knew he should pick her up and toss her into the black water below. It was his plan. It was her destiny. Yet despite every fiber of his being screaming at him to throw her over the edge, he couldn't bring himself to count to one.

The two of them stood on the bridge deck wrapped in each other's arms until the air grew cold. Eventually, without a word spoken, they headed back the way they came. Each of the lovers was thinking the exact same thing.

"I'll do it tomorrow."

ten

Henrik stared at the magazine rack until his eyes hurt.

A bookstore employee tapped him on the shoulder. "Excuse me, sir. May I help you?"

Henrik shook the cobwebs out of his head.

"No, thank you," he said.

The bookstore employee gave him a perturbed look and walked away. Henrik waited until the nosy employee was out of view and then grabbed six magazines, including one in a plastic wrapper from the back shelf, and walked into the coffee shop attached to the enormous bookstore.

A woman with blond highlights and chubby ankles was ahead of him in line.

"I'll have a venti iced caramel macchiato, add one and a quarter pump white chocolate and six pumps vanilla, go easy on the sixth pump, with two whole packets of Equal, no whip, cream foam and three dashes of cinnamon, one to start and two on top."

Henrik looked at her as though she was insane.

The barista called the woman's order and looked at Henrik to make his.

"I'll have a cup of coffee, black," he said.

"What size, sir?"

"Regular."

"We don't have size regular." The barista pointed up to the

list of prices on the wall. "We have tall, grande and venti."

The barista, a young woman of no more than nineteen, with short black hair, thick-rimmed glasses and an eyebrow ring protruding from a slightly infected patch of skin, shifted her stance from one leg to the other and glanced over Henrik's shoulder. Henrik looked back as well. A lineup had formed behind him. From the general look of displeasure on their faces, the six customers waiting in line seemed to be growing impatient.

It can't be this hard, Henrik thought. It's just ordering coffee.

"Whatever is the smallest, most regular size. That's what I'll have," he said.

Now the woman looked at him as though he was insane. She called out for a venti, charged him for a grande, and sent Henrik on his way.

Henrik sat down at a table by himself and flipped through the magazines. *Sports Fishing?* Didn't interest him. *Mobile Home Enthusiast?* It didn't catch his attention either. Henrik opened a martial arts magazine and read an article on the art of attacking a person with nunchucks. In the side panel were some truly awesome photos of a man dressed up as a ninja delivering a series of bone-shattering blows to his would-be attacker. The ninja was wearing a tight karate outfit that concealed everything except his eyes, while the attacker was dressed like a biker with a frayed jean jacket and a long goatee. Henrik noticed, and not for the first time, that bad guys in martial arts magazines and television programs typically have some sort of sinister-looking facial hair.

Henrik thought perhaps he could grow some facial hair, something to accentuate his woolly sideburns. A long ZZ

Top–like beard or a Fu Manchu moustache might go a long way in setting him apart from the rest of society. It would have been a perfect idea if not for the fact that Henrik could barely grow much more than a few gray whiskers at the bottom of his chin. His lack of hair growth — promoting testosterone was something of a blessing as Henrik wasn't really a facial hair kind of guy and besides, he'd long been annoyed by guys with goatees and backward baseball caps and didn't really want to look anything like them.

He was more fascinated by the man in the ninja costume. So fascinated in fact, that for approximately seven minutes, Henrik seriously considered taking up a martial art of some kind; not all nine disciplines one requires to become a full-fledged ninja, but perhaps a single martial art such as kickboxing or ninja star throwing — something that would involve less physical contact than judo. He pictured a scene from a movie involving an aerial overhead shot in which he, Henrik Nordmark, would dispatch a series of jean jacket–clad villains one by one. Some of his assailants would fall to his high-flying kicks and formidable punches. Others — those holding chains and two-by-fours with nails protruding from their ends — would drop to the ground clinging to their wounds, casualties of his astoundingly accurate ninja-star throwing. Yes, this all sounded great to Henrik.

His enthusiasm faded as he read the magazine further and learned that martial arts wasn't so much of an activity as it was a lifestyle and as un-athletic as Henrik was, he wasn't about to commit to starting an active lifestyle he knew he would most likely abandon in less than three weeks.

Henrik picked up the next magazine, the one in the clear plastic sheath, entitled *Naughty Neighbors*. The cover tantalized with salacious photos and blackened-out thumbnail images that suggested on the inside some neighbors were being quite naughty indeed. Henrik wasn't convinced. While the two girls in see-through brassieres on the cover were enjoying their bubble bath and appeared to be slightly badly behaved, he doubted very much that they lived next door to one another, or even in the same federal voting district.

He tossed the tantalizing rag aside and picked up a copy of *Maclean's*. On the cover was a picture of a young man slumped against a wall, smoking marijuana. The wall was held up by a stack of red and green poker chips. In large bold letters were the words "ADDICTION: A Revealing Exposé." Henrik got excited and flipped the magazine open. He read about all kinds of addictions — drug and alcohol, gambling addictions, sex addictions, internet and video games, even food addictions. It seemed like one could be addicted to just about anything.

A voice broke his concentration.

"Sir, have you purchased those magazines?"

The nosy bookstore employee had tracked Henrik down and was now intent on asserting some manner of authority over him.

"No, I haven't," Henrik said.

"Well you have to purchase items before you enter the coffee shop." The man pointed to a sign which read verbatim what he'd just said.

Part embarrassed, part indignant, Henrik looked down at the table and hoped the man would just go away. Eventually he did, but not before collecting the magazines Henrik had unintentionally absconded with. The bookstore employee gave Henrik a scolding look and slowly shook his head with disgust as he picked up the *Naughty Neighbors* magazine and then seemed to hover for a while, lording a supposed high moral standing over him. Henrik wanted to grab the man by the nose and yell, "*You* sell this magazine! You're equally culpable, if not more so, for selling this trash as I am for reading it!" But he couldn't find the internal fortitude to say anything and instead sat there sheepishly looking at a discarded packet of Sweet 'N Low on the floor until the man left.

Henrik sipped his black coffee and reflected on the addiction article. For all of the negatives associated with addiction, there was also something alluring about having a driving force in one's life. Gamblers lost their cars and houses to slot machines and blackjack tables and yet still they came back for more. Sex addicts caught all manner of STDs and exchanged phobia-breeding, germ-filled saliva with dozens if not hundreds of partners a year, yet still they cruised side streets and swingers bars desperate for someone to touch their private parts. The drug addict would rather steal than go without his fix.

Henrik longed to feel a compulsion so strong that nothing else mattered. He wasn't about to give up his job for a life of Dumpster diving and sticking needles in his arm. Nor was he willing to gamble away what little money he had on confusing table games in smoke-ridden casinos. But perhaps there was a way he could get close enough to one of these vices to tantalize his senses with just a taste of the pressing urge these people felt every day.

But which vice? That was the dilemma.

Henrik looked around for a sign — something, anything to help him decide. He searched the faceless faces passing by and hunted with his eyes along the walls. In the background, a song about three little birds played over the corporate bookstore stereo.

The sign appeared suddenly like a beacon on a dark night, one Henrik couldn't believe he'd overlooked. The entire bookstore tumbled down in his mind's eye, with people and bookshelves and cash registers collapsing by the wayside like trees run over by a bulldozer. The world disappeared and all that remained was a magazine on the next table — a copy of *High Times* with Bob Marley smoking a joint on the cover.

Henrik picked up the magazine and an insert fell out. He gazed at the 4x6 piece of orange paper with wide eyes and then tucked it discreetly in his pocket. Henrik stood up. In his haste, he knocked over his cup of coffee. It spilled off the edge of the table and burned the chubby ankles of the woman with the iced macchiato. He ignored his natural instinct to stop and apologize. Henrik walked out of the bookstore and into the street in search of euphoria. He was headed to the docks to buy himself some marijuana.

The docks were a scary place. Henrik had only ever been there on weekends and statutory holidays when the community fishermen's fair took over the area. He arrived to find a desolate wasteland of rusted cargo vessels, drunken hobos and random fish carcasses strewn across the pier. The Ferris wheel and cotton candy machines he anticipated, the families strolling around with little girls on their father's shoulders and boys pedaling Big Wheels, the all-ages fun and carnival games were absent. Even though it was well into the daylight hours, Henrik felt a dangerous foreboding about this place.

His mission was simple: purchase the marijuana and get the hell out of there in enough time to start work in an hour and fourteen minutes. He wandered around aimlessly for a while, careful not to make eye contact with any of the street people lurking in alleyways, before he saw a lone man sitting on a bench at the end of the pier. Henrik promptly walked over and introduced himself. The man had a long beard and a dark overcoat covered in fishing lures. His red face was partially hidden by his jacket and he didn't look up when Henrik said hello.

"Do you know where I might procure myself some Mary Jane?" Henrik said.

The man turned his head a fraction of an inch. His voice was whispery and full of needles.

"Do you mean a hooker?"

"Goodness no," Henrik said, flustered. "I'm looking for some grass. You know, some reefer."

The man stared straight through him. Henrik pulled the orange piece of paper out of his pocket. On this insert taken from the *High Times* magazine were all sorts of nicknames for the drug. Henrik's courage received an immediate boost as he was pretty sure he was less likely to get arrested if he spoke in code.

"Some Indonesian Bud. The Devil's Lettuce. You know, some Giggle Weed."

The man stood up slowly, with some effort. He was barely two inches taller than Henrik but in his dark cloak with its hundreds of hooks and lures, he towered in the air. "Giggle Weed?" the man said.

Henrik glanced around. The beach underneath the pier was deserted. There wasn't a single child building a sandcastle or a pair of lovers out for an early morning stroll. The wind whispered eerily in his ear and the rank smell of fish was coated in death. Henrik watched the water churn crisp against the dock and wondered how many bodies had washed up along this shore. Worse yet, how many hapless souls had been thrown to a watery grave from right here at this very spot? He stood absolutely still, too afraid to move.

"Yes," Henrik said. "Giggle Weed."

The man's mouth spread into a gray-toothed grin.

"We all buy our weed at the bait shop," he said.

Henrik followed the man's pointing finger with his eyes. He'd walked right by the bait shop and its Open for Business sign.

"Thank you, good sir," Henrik said and hurried off the pier as fast as he could.

Henrik entered the bait shop. A young girl was chewing bubble gum and standing behind a sign that read "Fifty Worms For Five Bucks."

"I would like to buy some Mary Jane," Henrik said. "And I don't mean a hooker. I mean Giggle Weed — marijuana or whatever the kids are calling it these days. I have seventeen dollars to spend."

The girl pulled a single joint out of her pocket and set it on the counter. She blew a pink bubble and let it pop before pushing the gum back into her mouth.

"That'll be seventeen bucks," she said.

Henrik tucked the marijuana into the breast pocket of his security guard uniform and headed to work. He was positively giddy, like a schoolgirl with a secret she was dying to share. He stood at his post nodding his head at the business-people who walked by, just as he'd done five days a week for the past twenty years. The only difference was the silly smile on his face. Occasionally when he thought nobody was looking, Henrik would place his hand over his pocket like Gollum cradling his precious ring.

When it came time for his break, Henrik practically skipped out the doors. He purchased a pack of matches for two cents at the local mini-mart and found a secluded spot behind the building. Henrik lit up the joint and took his first puff. He immediately coughed out loud. Not once or twice, but a few dozen times. Henrik shook his head in amazement at the dedication it must take to smoke several packs of cigarettes every day. One really had to commit to getting one's throat used to this corrosive pain.

He sucked in again and this time he inhaled the smoke deep into his lungs. It was sickeningly sweet, not enjoyable at all, and the worst part was, he didn't feel any different. Henrik polished off a full two thirds of the joint before he just couldn't take it anymore. He tossed the remains down a drain and stood beside the Dumpster waiting for the pot to take effect. One minute passed and then another. Henrik didn't feel different at all. The more time that went by, the more it appeared he was entirely immune to the effects of marijuana. Henrik instantly regretted the addiction he'd chosen and was busy making plans to try either irresponsible gambling or perhaps an incremental dependence on peach schnapps when he took a single step forward.

Henrik's foot felt as light as a feather. He took a second step and then a third. His legs, those short, stout tree trunks that had always affected his ability to play sports, suddenly filled with pins and needles. Henrik walked around, tentatively at first and then with confidence, his feet gathering momentum with each consecutive step. Henrik was truly amazed at this thing called walking. He imagined his ancestors from millennia ago, having crawled on all fours for centuries, finally discovering this mode of two-legged transportation and what a liberating feeling it must have been. Henrik felt as though he were walking on water. He glided along the surface like a back-alley Jesus while all manner of slippery eels and automaton fish swam underneath the concrete.

Had an outsider happened to walk by and spot Henrik at this exact moment, they would have seen the most peculiar sight — a bald, middle-aged security guard with a look of unrestrained glee on his face, skipping around the alleyway, swinging his arms and stopping every few seconds to look down and imagine what kind of aquatic vertebrate lived beneath his feet.

Henrik stopped abruptly to gaze up at the tall buildings. "Gravity," he said. "Gravity doesn't seem to be doing its job." Why were all these buildings standing tall in the city when gravity was so powerful it could pull meteors out of the sky? Shouldn't it have torn these skyscrapers down long ago? Concrete and pillars, glass windows, men in ties and women wearing pantsuits — all these things lived in the offices above and here dwelling on the land was Henrik Nordmark with his water balloon–shaped pot belly and ambitions to become unique. For the life of him, he couldn't imagine why things weren't constantly falling out of the sky.

He checked his watch. The face looked huge, like someone had strapped a wall clock to his wrist. It was time to head back.

Henrik took his post by the door and stood like a statue watching people go by. Even as he marveled at the strange sizes of their heads — some round, others bumpy, some that

seemed to be missing chins and still others that had fore-
heads like battering rams — he regretted that he had yet to
feel the pot take effect.

Henrik was lamenting the loss of seventeen dollars to
ineffective marijuana when suddenly the world slowed down
to a standstill. Like molasses, the businessmen and couriers
moved as though they were striving to climb steep hills.
Henrik wanted to help them, to run over and push them in
the small of the back. *You can make it to the elevator! Keep trying! All is not lost!* But Henrik couldn't move. He froze in
place, his mind occupied by whether or not he really had to
pee. He was counting how many times he'd used the lavatory
today when a police officer entered through the front doors.
This cop walked at a different pace than everyone else. His
stride was fast and hard, a hare leaving tortoises in his wake.
He extended his hand to Henrik.

"I'm Constable Sullivan."

Henrik stared at this man's formidable moustache.

"Security Guard Henrik Nordmark," he replied.

"We got a call from one of the merchants on the third floor.
The smell of marijuana smoke entered through their windows.
Usually we wouldn't investigate something like this but the
mayor introduced a new Say No To Drugs campaign just last
week and my sergeant's been on my ass."

Henrik's heart skipped a beat. He tried to swallow but the
saliva got lodged in his throat.

"How may I help?" he said.

The constable took off his hat and held it in his hands.
"Have there been any teenagers hanging around the building? Do any street people sleep out back?"

Henrik could barely catch his breath. A single bead of

sweat originated from somewhere atop his vast scalp and careened down his forehead. It was the first drop in a torrential downpour.

"No sir," he said. "No unruly teenagers or hobos."

The officer placed his hand on Henrik's shoulder and took him aside. "Are you all right?" he said. "Your face is all red and you're sweating pretty bad. You look like you're about to have a panic attack."

Henrik could barely pay attention to the man's words, so chaotic was the swell in his brain. He kept replaying a television commercial in his head from twenty years ago in which a man held an egg to depict the regular human brain and then cracked the egg into a frying pan to show what your brain looks like on drugs. Months after that commercial aired, a poster in the supermarket took the metaphor a step further by showing your brain on drugs with a side of bacon. After having only a fuzzy recollection of this poster for the past decade, Henrik suddenly thought it was the funniest thing he'd ever seen. He stifled a giggle. Henrik tried his best to hold in the rest but he laughed out loud in spite of himself.

The constable was still staring at him. Henrik needed an excuse. Not just any excuse, but a really good one that would both explain and mystify.

"I ate some bad roast beef this morning," he said.

"You have to take care of yourself, buddy," the cop said. "Get some fresh air and exercise." He tapped Henrik on the shoulder and walked out the front doors.

Henrik returned to his post and stood there for the rest of the day. At some point — he really wasn't sure when it happened — the marijuana wore off and only then did he realize how high he'd been. The remaining hours of his day were a torture session revolving around staring at the clock and counting the seconds as they passed. The minute hand labored as it clicked and Henrik felt the day would never end. When it finally did, he headed home with a strange compulsion to listen to the Beatles' *Sgt. Pepper* and eat a plate of bacon. Neither was immediately available so Henrik listened to what he thought was a Ringo Starr solo track on the radio and ate some green ham that had been sitting in his refrigerator for a month. The song turned out to be an unmelodic Elvis Costello B-side and the ham was convincingly inedible.

He passed out on the couch that evening, his head aching and his stomach in knots.

Henrik awoke with a start in the middle of the night. He stood up and walked in a zombie-like state to the bathroom where he found a sample-sized packet of expired Anacin in a drawer by the sink. Henrik popped the two little white pills in his mouth, shot them down with a glass of water and brushed his teeth by the open window. He looked up into the sky and took in the stars. They were bright tonight. Even the city lights couldn't obscure them. Had his eyes not been so tired, he could have stared up at the stars for hours. Henrik glanced at the clock on the wall. His shift at work started in six hours. He shut his blinds, the night sky disappeared and Henrik went to bed.

Across the city at that very moment, a young man was sitting on his windowsill, staring up at the same stars. He couldn't sleep, he was so excited. "I'm rich," he said to himself. "My life is going to change."

That young man's life was indeed about to change.

But not, as he would learn, for the better.

 eleven

The next morning, Roland headed to the office dressed in a T-shirt and a pair of casual Banana Republic pants. There was no way he was going to wear a suit on his last day at work. Besides, it was casual Friday and most of his clients would be wearing jeans. He walked up to his desk and sat down.

Mason's seat in the cubicle next to him was still conspicuously absent. Roland imagined Mason sitting on the company vice president's jet surrounded by gorgeous flight attendants, a cognac in one hand and a cigar in the other. Just days ago this image would have haunted him like no other. He would have been plagued by night sweats and bitter to the very core. But karma had risen and fallen like the tides and he barely gave Mason's empty chair a second look.

Taped to Roland's monitor was a note he'd left to remind himself to visit his grandmother. "All in good time," Roland said. He tossed the note into the recycling and started composing a resignation email addressed to the entire company:

> Dear Heartless Bastards,
> I won the lottery. I'm rich as fuck and I hope you all rot in hell . . .

He'd barely finished typing the first sentence when his phone rang. It was Kara, his girlfriend of several months. Kara was a nice woman, fairly pretty and quite capable of making small talk in any social situation. She would have been perfect for Roland if not for the fact that her occupation gave him the out-and-out willies. Kara worked in the city morgue as a mortician's assistant and her chief responsibility was to prep the deceased for autopsies. Just the thought of her stripping down dead bodies made Roland shudder. If that wasn't evidence enough that he should find a new girlfriend, there was a single incident that had been nagging in the back of his mind. A month ago Kara made a comment and waved her hand in front of her nose after Roland stunk up her bathroom. She'd had friends over and everyone started laughing at him as Kara loudly talked about the smell and how no one could enter the bathroom for the next hour. Roland knew his resentment was unreasonable — absurd, even — but he'd never quite been able to forgive her for the fuss she made.

"Hello?"

"Hi Roland, it's Kara."

"I know. I saw your name on the call display."

"Oh. Well, I just wanted to see if we were still on for dinner at Joalina's tonight."

"You see," Roland said, "the thing is that I won the lottery yesterday."

"Oh my God, Roland. That's fantastic!"

"Yes, it is."

"Everyone's going to be so excited. We can celebrate tonight."

"See, that's the other thing," Roland stammered a bit. "I was thinking maybe it's best, you know, if we stopped seeing one another for a while."

There was a momentary stunned silence on the other end.

"Wait . . . you want to *break up*? Why?" Kara said.

"Well, to be honest with you, I'm going to be really rich. I figured this might be my only chance to date a supermodel or an actress or something. Some girl who might not even talk to me if I wasn't super rich."

"You're telling me you want to trade up?!"

"Well, when you say it like that, it doesn't sound very good," Roland said.

"But that's what you want, isn't it?"

Roland cleared his throat. "I just thought it would be best to be completely honest with you about my intentions. That way we can still be friends."

Kara's voice grew suddenly angry.

"So you're telling me you would rather date someone who loves you for your money than me?"

"Um . . ."

"You superficial bastard! That's the shallowest thing I've ever heard."

Roland sighed. "I was hoping you would understand. Life is short. I might never get another chance to have sex with a supermodel."

"You can go to hell!"

"I'm sorry you feel that way," Roland said. "Try not to be upset. You know, my grandmother always says — you can't control the actions of others. You can only control your perspective in this world."

Kara slammed the phone down.

Roland hung up his phone as well and continued writing his email, all the while humming the tune to Kenny Rogers and Dolly Parton's "Islands in the Stream." He finished the note, signed it 'Roland the Rich' and was about to hit send when his supervisor Chad stopped by his desk.

"Roland, can I speak to you for a moment?"

"One second," Roland said. He scanned his email one last time, hit send and then turned back to Chad. "I'm all yours."

They walked down the hall to Chad's office. Chad shut the door behind them and the two men sat down in chairs facing one another. Chad was a full ten years older than Roland. He was also a good five inches shorter with a slighter build. Two years ago, during the period in which Roland grew his long unmanageable beard, Chad's curly black hair had started to recede. Chad headed his hairline off at the pass, abandoned his military-style crew cut and shaved his head. With his $500 Dolce & Gabbana glasses, his lightly starched shirts and his efficient bald head, he looked the part of confident success.

Roland didn't necessarily dislike Chad. He was an all right guy, Roland supposed. But he was corporate through and through. His blood flowed green with company money. Chad spoke in consulting speak — using phrases like *enabling vertical connectivity* and *re-engineering seamless paradigms*. Three months ago, Roland approached him with a legitimate business problem concerning one of their key clients. Chad hardly listened to Roland's issue before interrupting him and launching into a long-winded diatribe on how Roland should practice *leveraging synergies* in order to *ramp up a frictionless value chain*. Roland had given him a look of abject hatred, a look that Chad hardly seemed to notice. The past month had been, from Roland's perspective, tense to say the least.

Chad looked Roland square in the eyes.

"Roland," he said, "when you come into work in a

T-shirt, you send a certain message as to how you represent our company."

"But it's casual Friday," Roland said. In the background, he saw his email pop up on Chad's computer.

"Yes, it's casual Friday, but that only means we don't have to wear suits," Chad leaned back and let Roland have a good look at his pleated khakis and faded orange golf shirt. "You still have to wear something with a collar."

Roland lowered his eyes in a descending arc toward his torso where his navy blue T-shirt hugged his body. He looked back at Chad, who was nodding his head in self-acknowledgment of the synergies he was currently leveraging.

Chad continued. "I find it's best in these situations to look to someone with years of experience under his belt, someone with strong moral fiber, good family values and a keen eye for doing what's right for the business. I like to take a step back and ask myself — what would Regis do?" Chad gave Roland an expectant look. The room fell so suddenly quiet a pin drop would have sounded like a grenade. "Do we have an understanding?" Chad said.

"No," Roland said.

"What do you mean?"

"I mean — we don't have an understanding. I'm not going to come in here on casual Fridays wearing some god-awful golf shirt with a corporate logo on the breast pocket. I look good," he gestured toward his T-shirt. "You're the one who looks like an asshole."

Chad's relentless nodding came to a grinding halt.

"Excuse me?"

"You heard me," Roland said. "I won't comply. So fuck you. Fuck you and the horse you rode in on."

Roland leaned back in his chair and placed his hands behind his head in great satisfaction. An enormous weight instantly lifted off his shoulders. He was only seconds away from escaping this cubicle prison. All he had to do now was sit back and wait for Chad to fire him. Only Chad couldn't speak. His brain had slowed to a Neanderthal crawl. All of the courses Chad had been on — the company retreats with their PowerPoint presentations and their index cards and the uniformity of it all — hadn't prepared him for such brazen insolence. There wasn't a consulting phrase in his mental dictionary to apply to this problem. Luckily for Chad, he wouldn't have to say anything. At that exact moment, the company president showed up at Chad's door. He had two security guards with him and he looked angry. Apparently, he'd read Roland's email.

Two and a half minutes later, Roland was tossed out into the street and told never to return. The guards manhandled him a little on the way out, but Roland wasn't upset. In fact, he would have had it no other way. He struggled with the guards, yelled obscenities and cursed out the random pictures of company ambassador Regis Philbin on the walls. When they entered the elevator, Carol from accounting was just exiting. Roland told her she had really nice tits and that he'd always wanted to tell her that. Carol from accounting didn't seem to know how to take a compliment as she called Roland an asshole. Roland said, "If you want to see an asshole, go to Chad's office. There's an asshole for you."

He was then dragged through the lobby and made to leave not only the building, but the company property itself. On his way out through the lobby, a short bottom-floor security guard who looked vaguely like Alfred Hitchcock bore witness to Roland's antics and opened the doors for all three of them. Henrik watched in stupefied wonder. Now, *there's* a man who knows how to make an impression, he thought. He has such passion, such eccentricity, such commitment to his cause. No one will ever forget him. He'll be defined by this forever.

Henrik's heart sank to the bottom of his stomach as he watched Roland being dragged out into the street. Not in his wildest dreams could he ever behave that way. Or could he? Roland's wild taunts and flailing arms stirred within Henrik a sudden revelation.

When the guards from the fifteenth floor returned, Henrik informed them that he was feeling quite ill and asked if one of them would be so kind as to take his spot in the lobby for the rest of the day. The nicer of the two guards volunteered and Henrik left work early. He headed straight to the local shopping mall.

Outside, Roland couldn't contain his excitement. He felt so alive. For the first time in months — years even — he was excited about life. This money would change everything. It had to. He'd already dumped his girlfriend and quit his job. As well, there was at minimum a 90% chance that he no longer had any friends left. Every friend Roland had in this world worked at the company from which he'd just been fired and in his resignation email he called many of them out, making obscure references to long-forgotten incidents that Roland had never been able to let go.

In addition to the wicked insinuations he launched upon Mason, Roland charged Bradley from sales with never paying a proper tip in a restaurant, general frugality and altogether cheap behavior. He charged the computer guy Graham with leering at his mother's breasts, a crime made infinitely worse by her accidental death a mere three months after the incident of Graham's lustful eye. Roland indicted several others on even more malicious accounts — adultery, intentional cold spreading, silent farting during closed-door meetings and most egregiously, the malicious cock-blocking of Roland's attempts to seduce Carol's breasts at last year's Christmas party.

Roland had forsaken everything — love, employment, friendship. Undaunted, he walked down the street with a skip in his step. He would start over again. There was a new life to be had out there and he had enough money to buy it. He'd already arranged to go speed dating at an affluent restaurant in the downtown district. There he planned to meet a beautiful, alluring woman who would be impressed with his newfound wealth. Yes, the world was his oyster and Roland planned to suck all of the goodness out of it.

Roland's cell phone rang. He picked it up without looking at the number on the call display.

"Hello?"

"You bastard!"

"Mason, how are you on this fine day?"

"It's not how I am. It's where I am."

Roland stopped at a crosswalk. "And where's that?"

"Five minutes ago I was sitting in the corporate jet getting ready to take off to the Bahamas. Then the company vice president opens his laptop and checks his email. Next thing I know, he throws me off the plane and now I'm standing on a runway at the airport holding my suitcase and wondering what the hell happened."

"That's terrible," Roland said. "What an unfortunate turn

of events."

"Don't be a smart-ass," Mason said. "The vice president said you sent an email to the whole company. What did it say?"

Roland was momentarily distracted by a Spanish beauty with long flowing locks and a swivel in her hips. He stared at her miniskirt and Supergirl top until the light turned green. "In my email, I mentioned that you only got the job because you promised the interviewer you would dress up for him like Cher and sing 'If I Could Turn Back Time' with your pants off. I might also have mentioned that your new job title would be Oral Liaison to the Vice President."

"You didn't!"

"I did. And I also attached a few of the emails you've sent me over the years."

"Which ones?"

"Let me see, in one you said that the day Carol from accounting wore a tank top to the staff volleyball game was the best day of your life."

"That's not so bad. There's no way they would fire me for that," Mason said.

"In another one you wrote that our upper management is filled with a bunch of lazy miscreants who couldn't work a register at McDonald's. You also said the only way to take care of them would be to give each and every one of them an enema with a garden hose."

"I never wrote that."

"Oh yes you did. March fifteenth. Three years ago. The day you got passed over for a promotion for Chad's job. I saved the email in a special folder for just such an occasion."

"You son of a bitch! This is ten times worse than anything

I ever did."

Roland pumped his fist in the air, victorious.

"That may be true. But much like Rocky, I didn't draw first blood."

"That's Rambo, you idiot."

Roland stopped in front of the bank. "What?"

"Rambo was the one in *First Blood*. Rocky was in *Rocky*."

"Fascinating," Roland said. "Perhaps you can get a new job as a professional movie buff. Now listen, I have some really important things to do. But have a great day and a great life and take the time to enjoy yourself. You deserve it."

Roland hung up the phone and entered the bank. He removed his jeans from the safety deposit box and carried them all the way across town to the local lottery office. With confidence, he told the woman behind the counter that he'd just won the lottery. She seemed genuinely excited for him and called out to her supervisor. Very carefully, in full view of three lottery officials, Roland pulled the ticket from the back pocket of his jeans and couldn't believe his eyes. His entire world — the fictional one he'd built up in his mind in which he was a jet-setting vagabond playboy with two girls on either arm and an arsenal of rock star friends — came crashing down to painful reality.

The white ticket, smudged with a little plum juice, contained the numbers 1, 2, 3, 4, 5, 6.

 twelve

Conrad knocked on the door. On the other side, a motion sensor flashed a red light to alert Billy Bones that he had visitors. Conrad slammed his fist against the door a second time. When there was no answer, he and Alfred both frowned. Their stone deaf associate Bones might merely have passed out in his Barcalounger. But at Shady Oaks Park, where any nap in front of the television could be your last, an unanswered knock at Bones' door more likely meant one of three things: (1) he'd keeled over and was lying in a puddle of drool on the linoleum floor, (2) he'd finally cornered the young floor nurse and was blissfully chasing her around his room or (3) he'd grown so delirious he'd forgotten how to use the doorknob.

"Bones!" Conrad yelled. "Get a move on, old chap."

Silence filled the hall. Conrad twirled the ends of his moustache with his gloved hand while Alfred picked at a liver spot on top of his head.

"Perhaps we'll be completing the mission ourselves," Conrad whispered under his breath.

"Gentlemen," a voice called from down the hall. "Gentlemen, may I help you?"

The voice came from the retirement home director, one Abraham Arnold, formerly executive administrator of the esteemed Cottage Estates. At fifty-one years of age —

decades younger than Conrad and his associates — Abraham was all business. He ushered the residents around like cattle and chased down the sick and decrepit the way a shady lawyer chases ambulances. Abraham saw each resident who died as yet another room he could rent at a higher rate. And the residents knew it. They nicknamed him the Grinning Reaper, in part because of his appearance — his lofty height, his far-too-large head that swiveled as if on a pendulum, and his hunched over, Lurch-like demeanor — but more for the ominous way he stood beside the gurneys of recently deceased seniors with barely an effort made to conceal his gleeful smile or the dollar signs in his eyes.

Some of the more paranoid residents had suggested Abraham kept toe tags in his suit pocket and others remarked on his somewhat clairvoyant ability to sense when a resident had fallen down and broken a hip. To a person, they all feared Abraham.

Everyone, that is, except Conrad.

Three months earlier, Conrad had had enough of Abraham's imperial rule and hired a private investigator to dig up dirt on the retirement home director. And such dirt there was! Abraham's son, it turns out, was a high school dropout with dreadlocks and a bong in his back pocket. His wife Bianca (nicknamed Bunny in social circles and Pickle by her Scandinavian lover) spent her evenings guzzling boxes of red wine and busied her days spending Abraham's money on antidepressant-fueled shopping binges.

Most scandalous of all was Abraham himself. Only recently he'd taken over at Shady Oaks Park after being released from his contract at the released from his contract at the much-vaunted Cottage Estates, largely considered the Rolls Royce of retirement homes. Sizeable amounts of money were alleged to have disappeared into a tangled web of holding companies and offshore bank accounts. While it was never proven, Abraham remained the chief suspect.

Conrad had been biding his time, waiting for the perfect moment to make the tall man wither in his presence. "We're just waiting for our associate to answer his door," Conrad said.

Abraham drew nearer. Conrad could smell him now.

"You needn't hover," Conrad said. "I'm sure everything is fine. Bones will be out in a moment."

"Are you sure? I could use my master key to unlock the door."

Conrad held up a gloved hand.

"You will do nothing of the sort."

"Nonsense," Abraham moved toward the door.

"How is that son of yours?" Conrad said. "You know, the titan of industry. What is he again? A stockbroker on Wall Street?"

Abraham stopped short.

"He's a stock boy at Walmart. You know perfectly well —"

A smile curled at the corner of Conrad's mouth.

"And how about your wife? Bunny's her name? Or is it Pickle?"

Abraham went white. He shoved his keys back into his jacket.

"Do tell me good sir, what is the Scandinavian word for pickles?" Conrad said.

Alfred, delighted to see the Grinning Reaper squirm, attempted to get in on the banter. A clever quip — involving raw cucumbers, the pickling process and Abraham's wife's non-virginal womanhood — formed at the tip of his tongue but never fully left his mouth. As Conrad struggled to hear what his associate was saying, Abraham mustered his courage.

"Where are you taking Mr. Bones this morning? Does this have anything to do with that man who visited the other day? The man in the red suit?"

Just then the door swung inward and Billy Bones appeared in his three-piece suit, smelling vaguely of mothballs. He stared blankly at the three men standing in the hallway.

"Billy!" Conrad said loud enough for his counterpart to hear. "What took you so long?"

"I was applying my cologne. Now let's go find the target —"

"Tut-tut," Conrad moved to place his blind hand over Billy's mouth. He fumbled a little and poked Billy in the eye but nonetheless managed to stop his associate from talking. "Beware of prying ears," he motioned in what he assumed was Abraham's direction.

Billy gazed up at Abraham as though he was seeing him for the first time. He took a good long look, tilted his neck to either side to examine the tall man and then stepped back.

"You sure got a strange head on you," he said.

Abraham, already flustered by Conrad, could only mutter his response. "I'm just as God made me, sir."

"Ah yes," Conrad said. "The maker truly did break the mold on that fine day."

Alfred reached in and shut Bones' door. Conrad twirled his cane. And Billy trudged down the hall ahead of the pack. They made it thirty feet before Abraham finally noticed the metal briefcase in Alfred's hand. He called out.

"I'll find out what you're up to! Whatever it is, I assure you — you won't get away with it!"

His voice faded as they rounded the corner. The three elderly assassins, carrying a case loaded with ammunition, were off to find Henrik Nordmark.

thirteen

Henrik realized he could never truly be a saint. He tried chivalry long ago and found it to be an abstract notion that was nearly impossible to accomplish in reality. He knew he would never do great things that made people speak of him with admiration. But watching that young man get thrown out of the office building made Henrik realize you don't have to be good to be distinct or unique. An equal effect can be achieved by being bad. Henrik walked to the local shopping mall intent on becoming a public menace. It was easy, he decided. He would simply mimic the actions he found most deplorable in others. One could much more readily inspire hatred than love. Some day, he reasoned, he might grow out of aberrance. But for now, it was the first step along a diving board into a pool of eccentricity.

Once inside the shopping mall, Henrik proceeded to walk through the stores and haphazardly rearrange the clothes folded on the shelves. He would pick up an article — a T-shirt or a cardigan, a pair of pleated pants or a lady's full bodice — it didn't really matter what it was — and he would crumble it in his hands and unfold its sleeves, then place it back indiscriminately on the shelf. With each piece of clothing, Henrik imagined himself to be more and more wicked, a certifiable brute in this world. He furnished a demonic cackle, far too quiet for anyone to hear, but loud enough to underscore the depravity of his actions.

To Henrik's immense dismay, the store staff didn't seem to notice. He'd anticipated at least one of them would grow furiously angry and throw him out of the store on his heels. But none of them seemed to care. In one store, a young man wearing women's jeans and a pink headband even followed along behind Henrik, dutifully cleaning up his mess and making small talk with him.

Henrik would have to up the ante.

He found the most crowded hallway in the mall and set about walking slowly and taking up as much space as he possibly could. *This will do the trick*, he thought. Many a time while walking down a busy city sidewalk, Henrik had found himself victim to the incredible scourge of slow, overweight women meandering along at a breathtakingly unhurried dawdle, their leisurely attitude and seeming obliviousness to the traffic jam behind them causing a rage to form deep within Henrik to where it manifested in a tightness in his chest. They always traveled in flocks, these women. Henrik had no such flock, but still, he set about eliciting an angry response from the shoppers in the mall. He waddled four times slower than normal, stretched out his arms and stumbled absently in people's way when they attempted to pass him. To Henrik's horror, his actions had little effect. No one seemed to notice him in the least. He was only one man after all and the shoppers could pass him easily on either side. Henrik increased his efforts and slowed down to a skulking crawl. He was almost standing still now. This made it even easier for the shoppers to garner passage along the crowded corridor. Henrik heaved a great sigh. This process, he realized, necessitated their being at minimum two meandering loafs. He could never achieve this alone.

Dismayed, Henrik headed to the food court in a last-ditch attempt to be hated by all.

Once inside the food court, he sat down in a crowded area next to the New York Fries and took off his shoe, followed by his sock, which he waved in the air dramatically for all to see. He then produced a pair of nail clippers from his pocket and began clipping his toenails one by one. He started with the second toe. It had a jagged, thick nail stricken with cavernous yellow craters and sharp edges on either side. It would need two attacks with the clippers at minimum, perhaps as many as six. Henrik dug in hard. Clip! A piece of nail shot straight from his toe and landed several feet away next to a family of four. They didn't even look up from their soup. Undaunted, Henrik dug in again and chopped away at the toenail as though he was felling a great redwood in the forest. Clip! Clip! Clip!

Randomly, outrageously, pieces of toughened keratin flew from the end of his animal digit. With a devilish smile, Henrik dug into his middle toe and proceeded to obliterate its nail as well. He looked up from his work to discover the entire food court was oblivious to his actions. How could this not bother them? It would be driving Henrik crazy! He was already angry, but now grew even further incensed at the fact that he was outraged and they were not. Henrik returned to his undertaking with even more purpose. He chopped away at the other toenails before he reached his Everest — the big toe. His anger fled as he thought about all the quantifiable adjectives people in the food court might use to describe him when pieces of the big nail went flying; words like deplorable, heinous, unhygienic. True, in a perfect world he would rather be described in positive terms, with admirable, respectable and sanitary as the adjectives of the day. But this was not a perfect world. This was a prison in which Henrik had lived far too long in the solitary confinement of dreary dullness. He attacked his big toe in stages, chopping away first at the thick, difficult yellow sector on the left. Once free of this section, the rest of the toenail surrendered. But Henrik would show no mercy. He hacked away without remorse, caught pieces of nail in the air and threw them across the room. One fragment landed in the TacoTime salad of a woman sitting directly across from him.

Eureka! Henrik exclaimed inwardly. This poor victimized woman would finally notice his appalling behavior. She would be forced to stand up in the crowd and scream at him. She would arouse the attention of the others and classify Henrik as an outright scoundrel.

But the woman didn't notice the nail land in her salad. She continued eating, chatting all the while with her friend about Marc Anthony and how one day Jennifer Lopez would rip his heart out through his ass. Henrik watched in stupefied wonder as the woman ate every last bit of her salad. Together the two women stood up and walked away, leaving their trays on the table. Henrik hobbled over on one shoe and looked in the salad bowl. The woman had scraped it clean. There was no trace of the toenail. It could mean only one thing — Henrik's nail was at the bottom of that woman's stomach, swirling around with the Diet Coke and the taco meat.

Henrik felt himself about to vomit. He struggled to pull on his shoe and as he finished tying his laces, Henrik bent over and held his chest, determined not to deposit the contents of his stomach into the lady's salad bowl.

Just then, an arrow sailed straight over his head and struck a poor Dunkin' Donuts employee right in the chest. Henrik didn't even see it happen. Quickly a crowd rushed to the man's aid. *This is a tragedy!* they cried — although not nearly as great a tragedy as one might think. Only one week prior, the injured man had cheated on his wife with the teenage girl selling hot dogs at Orange Julius. He propositioned the hot dog girl outside a storage closet in the back hallway and then hammered away at her ruthlessly in the same closet, exited the moment he orgasmed and never spoke to her again. Until this moment his actions had gone unpunished.

That he was not entirely innocent would have been of small comfort to the three old men hiding behind the coffee kiosk across the way.

"Did we get him?" Conrad whispered to Billy Bones.

Billy was busy tucking the crossbow back in the briefcase. "What?!" he yelled.

"I asked did we get him?" Conrad said louder.

"No!" yelled Billy Bones. "We shot some other guy instead!"

"Keep quiet, you damned fool," Conrad swatted Billy Bones across the face with his glove. But Billy would not keep quiet. His senility was increasing exponentially by the hour. He yelled at Conrad, "Don't be mad at me! Alfred's the one who shot him!"

Faces in the crowd turned away from the ailing man and began searching for the source of the arrow. Their eyes focused on the area where the three elderly assassins were now ducking behind the coffee kiosk.

"I think we should take our leave," Alfred said inaudibly.

"What?!" Billy Bones yelled again.

"I think we should take our leave." Alfred slammed his fist on the kiosk in outrage that no one was listening to him.

Conrad stood up. "Now, Bones!" he screamed. "Now!"

Billy Bones stood up as well and looked down at the wheelchair the elderly assassins had brought with them. Unsure what to do, he stared back at his blind associate, his mind occupied by puppies and rainbows, the lifelong quest for fine bourbon and long-legged women in scanty attire. Conrad swung his cane wildly in the direction of Billy's leg, missed the shin bone entirely and caught him right on the ankle. The sudden stab of pain shot Billy out of his senile musings. He collapsed in a heap in the wheelchair.

"Step aside," Conrad said to the growing crowd. "This man requires immediate medical attention."

Alfred looked down to discover Billy Bones wasn't entirely acting. He'd already fallen asleep in the chair. Alfred grabbed the handles and started pushing. Conrad took his arm and they fled — well, rather they slowly shuffled — through the crowd with Alfred steering, Conrad swinging his cane to clear a path and Billy Bones snoring as though he'd fallen asleep in front of his black and white television.

Henrik stood in the middle of all of this, completely baffled. He couldn't quite see the man in the cape and his two associates make a bungling — though surprisingly successful — exit past Banana Republic and off into the distance. And he wasn't really sure what happened to the man lying on the ground. There were two crowds, one watching the elderly men make their escape and another huddled around the severely wounded Dunkin' Donuts employee, and neither of them were congregated for Henrik.

Henrik frowned a sad frown and left the food court.

In the aftermath, no witnesses had any idea what had happened. They hadn't noticed anyone in the food court acting strangely. Even Conrad's cape was a detail that slipped the minds of those interviewed. The only witness who could positively identify the assassins was the teenage girl from the hot dog stand at Orange Julius. But she didn't say a word. She couldn't speak. She was too busy trying to wipe the smile off her face.

 fourteen

Discouraged that after all his hard work, he remained entirely unnoticed, Henrik wandered over to a convenience store, bought an orange Shasta and a package of gummy bears and sat down on the curb to lament his fate by consuming as much sugar in as short a time span as possible. He wolfed down the gummy bears and choked back the soda. In the midst of his sugar high, Henrik watched the cars go by and wondered what to do next.

As the sugar wore off, Henrik reached into his pocket and found the toll-free number for Jacksonville's Religious Crusade. He'd written it down the other night and kept it with him in case of emergency. Henrik headed to the nearest pay phone and dialed the number.

There was a long pause before a woman with a southern accent answered.

"Hello, this is Betty Sue. Would you like to donate to Jacksonville's Religious Crusade?"

Henrik was deeply disappointed not to hear Parminder's voice.

"I'm looking for the woman I spoke to the other night," he said.

"Well, I can help you now, sir. How much would you like to donate? Do you have your credit card ready?"

"I think I'd really rather talk to the same woman from the

other night," Henrik said.

"Please hold," the woman said and then placed Henrik on hold before he could say Parminder's name. A Muzak version of the theme song from *Who's the Boss?* sounded over the line. Henrik waited through two verses and half a chorus before the signal abruptly cut dead. Undeterred, he immediately dialed again.

"Hello, this is Betty Sue. Would you like to donate to Jacksonville's Religious Crusade?"

"Hi Betty Sue, this is Henrik Nordmark. We just spoke. You were going to look for the woman I was speaking to the other night."

Betty Sue exhaled an audible groan.

"Sir, there are dozens of service representatives in our office. Do you know the name of the representative you spoke with?"

Henrik racked his brain for the alias Parminder had used. "It began with an M . . . Mary, I think."

"One moment please."

Henrik waited through a painful version of the *Leave It to Beaver* theme song, hoping the line wouldn't go dead again, before the music suddenly cut short and a second voice came on the line.

"Hello, this is Mary Jo. Would you like to donate to Jacksonville's Religious Crusade?"

Henrik was elated. "Is this Parminder?"

"I'm sorry sir, but there's no one here by that name."

"It's me, Henrik," he said. "We talked just the other night about Nanak and the Janamsakhis."

"Henrik, it's good to hear from you again!" Parminder's Indian accent returned in full force. "How are you? Have you found what makes you unique?"

"No. It's actually proven much more challenging than I anticipated."

"That's too bad."

Henrik leaned against the phone. He'd initially intended to ask her about the dinosaurs and how the millions of years they spent roaming the planet fit into Nanak's big plan for humankind. Henrik quickly forgot about that and became overjoyed at the idea of some random small talk. "How are things over there in India?"

"I went to see the monthly baby drop today," Parminder said.

"What's that?"

"It's a tradition in India. We all crowd around a big temple. The elders take newborn babies and drop them from the top of the temple."

"Do they land on the ground?!"

"Very rarely," she said. "Some men at the bottom hold a small sheet really tight so the babies bounce when they land. Then another man catches them in midair and hands them back to their mother. The tradition is supposed to promote strength in the child."

Henrik looked down at the ground. He could hardly believe that through the layers of cement and dirt, through the thick rock and past the Earth's molten core, there were people on the other side of the world who actually did this.

"How far do the babies fall?"

"About fifty feet or so."

"Isn't that kind of dangerous?"

"Yes," Parminder said. "Very much so."

"Has a baby ever missed the sheet and landed on the

ground?"

"Once or twice."

"Were they hurt?"

"Quite severely," Parminder said. "But at least my family has health insurance in case one of our babies gets injured and needs medical attention."

"Does the Jacksonville Religious Crusade pay your health insurance?"

"No. But because I'm a Sikh, I can buy my own."

Henrik was confused. "Because you're a Sikh?"

"Yes," she said. "Muslims, at least the really devout ones, can't buy health insurance because the Qur'an forbids gambling and Sharia law has deemed that buying insurance of any kind is a form of gambling."

Henrik thought back to when he was almost hit by the car. "I have health insurance. If I was maimed in some kind of accident and needed to be kept alive on a ventilator, my insurance carrier would pay for it."

"Would you really want to be kept alive on a ventilator?"

Henrik paused. What was the difference, he wondered, between his everyday life and being kept alive by a machine with tubes coming out of every orifice in his body? True, the able-bodied Henrik got up every day and went to work. And there were some joys in life — he liked to read the morning paper and look at the pretty girls as he walked down the street. In addition to the sugar he just ingested into his system, Henrik also enjoyed the occasional nearly ripe plum. But was this it? Was this everything that life held for him? The monotonous waking and eating and sleeping and waking? There had to be more to life than this. There just had to be.

"I want to be unique," he said. "I want to be an enema."

"Don't you mean an enigma?"

"What's the difference?"

"From my understanding, an enigma is a person who is something of a mystery. An enema is when they insert liquid into your bum to treat constipation."

"Do I have to choose between the two?"

"Henrik, my friend," Parminder said. "You can be anything you want to be. You can be as interesting and unique as you choose. You just have to find your own path."

"But that's my problem. I don't know which path I should take. I tried being a public menace and it turned out horribly. What should I do next?"

"You must not fall headlong into hopeless misery. Instead of beginning your quest with evil, perhaps you might start with virtue. Did you know that the gods favor those who are kind to the elderly?"

"Really?"

"Yes. Very much so."

Parminder proceeded to go on for over ten minutes about how the gods are pleased by those who show kindness toward the grayest and oldest of people. She knew it for a fact. Just as Allah commanded Muhammad Ali to beat up George Foreman and Jesus told Tammy Faye to wear lots of makeup and also told George W. Bush to invade Iraq, Nanak told her that young people who help the elderly are deemed virtuous in the eyes of others.

At the fifteen-minute mark, the phone line abruptly went dead. Henrik suspected it had something to do with Jacksonville's Religious Crusade having established a finite time limit for calls that don't result in donations. Or perhaps the Ab Lounger Deluxe people installed a time-sensitive algorithm to ensure their employees don't chat too long on the phone. It didn't matter. Parminder had told him all about honesty, integrity and being virtuous. He liked the sound of that word — virtuous.

Henrik headed down the street, armed with a determination to become virtuous and by definition, a much more interesting and unique person than he had been just hours ago.

 fifteen

Roland was trying to explain to his grandmother exactly what happened.

"But I don't understand," she said. "Why wouldn't you look at the ticket right away when you saw the numbers in the newspaper?"

"I don't know," Roland said, his eyes red from crying. In a few short hours, his skin had turned a pale, sickly white color.

"What about that nice girl you've been seeing, the one who paid for lunch at Denny's that time? What does she think of all this?"

"Kara?"

"Yes, that's it. Kara." Roland's grandmother leaned in close and turned on her wise-old-sage voice. "You know, you'll never do better than her."

Roland slouched in his chair.

"We broke up."

"What? Why?"

"It's a long story," he said. "Besides, she works with dead bodies. Part of her job is to take off their clothes when they arrive at the morgue. It really freaked me out."

"Any job that pays well for hard work is a worthwhile venture," Roland's grandmother said. She shook her head in condemnation. "Nothing you've done makes any sense. You're very impractical and impulsive sometimes."

"I know, Grandma. I know," Roland said. He had come to the old age home seeking consolation but had found little of it from his grandmother. Roland stood up to leave, only to realize he had nowhere to go.

"Let's look at this practically," his grandmother said. "What have you lost? You lost a job and a girlfriend and a few friends at work."

"It's not just what I lost," he said. "It's the way that I lost them. I got so caught up in thinking about what it would be like to be rich that I acted like a total asshole . . ."

"Watch your language."

". . . I acted like a total jerk and now I've got nothing."

"That's not true. You still have your health. And you still have your skills. What is it you do again?"

"I'm a business analyst, Grandma."

"Yes, you still have your business analyst skills. Why don't you just go back home and spend the afternoon trying to find a new job? There must be all sorts of businesses out there that need analyzing. I'll bet you find a job in a jiffy. Someone will be sure to hire a sweet boy like you."

Roland placed his head in his hands and broke into tears. He couldn't return to his apartment. He couldn't find a new job in some other cubicle dungeon. Didn't she understand that the moment he saw those winning numbers in the newspaper, his life had changed irrevocably? He could never go back to the way it once was — to being normal and poor and living paycheck to paycheck.

A member of the kitchen staff brought Roland's grandmother her fruit plate for dinner. She looked down at the kiwi and cantaloupe with delight and didn't understand why Roland couldn't do the same.

In the distance, Henrik entered the retirement home. He told the receptionist that he would like to read to the old people.

She gave him a funny look and asked him why.

Henrik responded that the elderly are society's treasures and they should be treated as such.

The easily fooled receptionist smiled and tilted her head a little. She informed Henrik that the residents were eating in the dining hall and that he could read to them after dinner. In the meantime, he was welcome to sit at a table and converse with anyone he wished. She handed him a copy of *Moby Dick*, a pencil and a piece of paper and sent him on his way.

Henrik shook her hand profusely before entering the dining hall. Upon seeing the populace, Henrik immediately had reservations about talking to them. They were all very gray and very old. Henrik suddenly remembered that as a child he was often afraid of old gray people. At the age of five, Henrik had two grandparents, one on either side of the family. His paternal grandfather was a frail old man with a set of wooden dentures that worked in conjunction with his two remaining teeth, a single yellow incisor at the top of his mouth and a blackened molar along the lower ridge. His maternal grandmother, with her sporadic halitosis exacerbated by a love for French onion soup, was equally challenged in the areas of dental hygiene. Young Henrik never understood why his Granny and Grandpapa lived apart. He assumed that since they'd both lost their partners, they would take up a romance with one another. In addition to curing any residual loneliness, such an arrangement would have made holidays and special occasions much more convenient for Henrik and his parents. This union very well might have worked had Henrik's grandparents not fought like cats and dogs every time they were together. These arguments would often devolve into screaming matches, at which point a frightened young Henrik would take refuge under his mother's floral dress.

Henrik gazed around the room. These old people weren't nearly as scary in person as they were in theory. In general, they looked just like the people from the food court, only a great deal shorter and much closer to death. Henrik noticed that the defining characteristic of the elderly is the pride they take in their ear and nose hair. At least, Henrik reasoned, they must be proud of these hairs in order to display them so prominently. Everywhere he looked there were thick clusters of wiry gray hairs sticking out of noses and wax-filled cobwebs collecting in peoples' ears. It wasn't a phenomenon restricted by gender either. Both men and women displayed these with equal vanity. Henrik reached up and touched his own ears. He felt suddenly ashamed of how hairless and clean they were.

The elderly were eating in groups at the tables. Had there been an old pensioner sitting on his own, Henrik might have sat down with him. Instead, he sat at a table by himself along the side wall and flipped open *Moby Dick*. He felt no guilt for sitting alone. Talking about the weather with these strangers would have been slightly more virtuous than he'd intended his first time out. He would start by reading to them, see if that made him any more pious or unique, and if it did not, he would try making small talk with them next time.

In the far corner closest to the kitchen, blind Conrad and mute Alfred were eating their supper and secretly nursing their pride after the failed assassination attempt. Alfred spotted Henrik right away. His eyes nearly popped out of his head when he saw him. Alfred tried to get the attention of his associates but Conrad was busy searching his string beans for signs of tampering and Billy Bones was off in the distance, having a particularly in-depth conversation with the floor nurse.

"You know I'm not going to do that," she said.

"You showed them to Karl down the hall last December."

"Yes," the nurse said, "but he gave me a two-thousand-dollar tip for Christmas."

Billy squinted and a large wrinkle formed along the bridge of his nose.

"What? I didn't hear you."

"Are you going to give me two grand?" the nurse said.

"Of course not!"

"Why don't you go down the hall after dinner?" she said. "Mrs. Komick will show you hers for free."

"But her breasts are eighty-six years old."

"And mine are twenty-six years old. And they'll cost you."

Alfred hurried toward the corridor by the kitchen where Bones and the nurse were standing. He grabbed Billy's arm to get his attention. Billy tried to ignore him and when Alfred kept tugging on his sleeve, Billy shot him an angry glare. "I'm getting somewhere here," he said, somewhat slyly.

"Look!" Alfred yelled. It came out as an inaudible whisper.

The nurse turned and walked her twenty-six-year-old body into the kitchen.

Billy Bones glanced around aimlessly. His senility had increased by at least eighteen percent since the incident in the food court a few hours ago. Alfred grabbed Billy's head and pointed it toward the far wall where Henrik was sitting in his security guard uniform, quietly flipping through *Moby*

Dick. Billy Bones' eyes lit up like lightbulbs. The two old-timers hustled over to their table, bumping into each other along the way. When they finally reached their fearless leader, Billy cupped his hands together and hollered into Conrad's ear.

Conrad reeled slightly from the noise and then his expression turned serious. He pulled his black gloves tight against his hands.

"Gentlemen," he said, "it appears we have a rooster in the hen house."

While staring at the copy of *Moby Dick* lying on the table, Henrik was reminded why he'd never been a great lover of literature. It seemed to him to be a very time-consuming activity and one you would have to excel at in order to truly distinguish yourself as an expert. And even then, you were merely an expert on the recorded thoughts of someone else, not the bearer of your own creation. Henrik read the name Herman Melville and played with the vowels so they rolled off his tongue. He wondered — how did this Herman fellow know he was unique enough to write a novel, and not just any novel, but a great classic of modern literature? Was it something he was born with? Or did Mr. Melville's novel come to him as a sudden inspiration? If the latter, what was the source of that inspiration? Opium? The word of God speaking to him in his dreams? A combination of the two?

Perhaps I can write a novel, Henrik thought. How hard could it be? He opened *Moby Dick* and flipped through the pages. Just glancing at the sheer volume of the work, it appeared to be exceedingly difficult after all. Just think of how much work it would be to eliminate all of the typos. He knew he could never complete such an undertaking. And besides, there existed in Henrik a deep-seated fear that were he ever to complete a novel, his work might be considered mere pulp fiction and thrown in with such non-artistic sorts as Clive Cussler and Danielle Steel. He could spend years working on a book containing what he felt were intricate plot twists and brilliantly developed characters only to be labeled generic by a harsh and unsympathetic public. If only there was a shorter, quicker way to self-expression and inner enlightenment.

I know, Henrik thought. *I'll write a poem.*

Poetry was a much better creative outlet for several reasons. First, it could be as short as a few lines and still be taken seriously. Moreover, a poem could be abstract and it didn't necessarily have to follow any specific structural rules. That was definitely a plus. And most important of all, it didn't really have to make any sense. A poem, Henrik decided, was a work of art by definition.

Henrik took out a blank piece of paper and waited for inspiration to strike but found his muse reticent, tired and truth be told, more or less functionally retarded. He started to write a poem about how difficult it is to write a poem before remembering that an article in the Arts and Life section of last Sunday's newspaper had described such poems as not only the last endeavor of the uncreative mind, but also utterly insipid and patently boring. *Boring*. Exactly what Henrik meant to avoid. Henrik dropped his pen in languid frustration.

He thought himself about to cry and decided inwardly what a great thing it would be to cry in this retirement home in front of all these people. They would see by his outward showing of sadness that on the inside he was a deep, brooding soul — mysterious even — one so devastated by the ways of this world that he was compelled to throw decorum to the wind and break down in public in a torrential sea of aching tears. Henrik grew excited by this notion . . . so excited that his welling eyes instantly dried up and he forgot entirely why he'd wanted to cry in the first place.

"Mr. Nordmark." A tall man with a towering forehead tapped Henrik's shoulder and introduced himself as the retirement home director. Henrik snapped his head back as though he'd come out of a trance. The dark circles around this man's eyes were startling. With the grayish hue to his skin and his jet black suit, he looked more like an undertaker than a caregiver for the elderly.

"It's time to read to the residents now," the tall man said.

He led Henrik up to a small stage in the corner of the dining hall. A piano took up most of the performance area, but there was a chair for him at the edge of the stage. He sat down and about a third of the seniors shuffled over and took their seats.

Henrik looked them all in the eyes. No one made a sound. He flipped the book open to the first page and stared at the first sentence. This novel appeared to be about a man named Ishmael who really enjoyed sailing. While Henrik expected something entirely different from the deceiving title, he nevertheless thought he might enjoy reading this book about pirates.

Henrik read the first paragraph out loud. It was all going exceedingly well when a sudden orange surge of anxiety lurched up from his stomach into his chest and took root firmly in the base of his throat. Henrik looked up at the elderly expectant faces and then down at the page again. The words and sentences, which moments ago had appeared in perfect symmetrical order, now looked like the crumbled keys of a broken piano. Henrik felt that if he tilted the book to the side, the letters would slip off the page and collapse into a pile at his feet.

Deep inside, he knew this was illogical. This was a book — bound paper, cardboard and glue — nothing more and nothing less. It could have been stage fright that held him motionless. Henrik's television had told him about the devastating effects of stage fright before. No one was immune, not even great thespians with multiple performances of Shakespeare under their belts. It even affected rock gods like Ronnie James Dio.

More likely Henrik's predicament arose from the idea that by reading to these old people, he might actually become virtuous and, as a byproduct, unique. That the end of his journey was finally within arm's reach frightened him to his core. Henrik couldn't shake the feeling that if he lifted a single page, the world would collapse around him.

Through sheer force of will, Henrik read another sentence out loud. An audible sigh of relief sounded from the gathering of grandmas and grandpas who had been watching this bald man stare at the book in silence for nearly two minutes. Henrik read a second sentence but only got through the first three words before Roland began wailing out loud on the other side of the room. A couple of nurses headed over to make sure he was okay and a crowd of old ladies formed around him. Henrik tried to peer past the women and get a good look at who was crying but he couldn't see Roland through the assembly line of concerned faces. He grew instantly jealous of the attention the young man was receiving. Sympathy and compassion were much more inviting than suffering through this shoddy recital. Had Henrik not grown so excited at the thought of crying, thus negating his tears just minutes ago, it would have been him surrounded by the gaggle of women. Henrik stood up and slammed the book down on the chair.

"I'll be right back," he said and headed straight to the bathroom to have a bowel movement.

From a crack in the open doorway, Alfred and Billy Bones watched Henrik walk down the hallway and enter the public lavatory. Quickly, they shut the door and reported their findings to Conrad. The leader of the assassins twirled the ends of his moustache with fingers covered in black leather gloves.

"Gentlemen, I think we've been discovered," Conrad said.

"That's impossible," Alfred mouthed without making a sound.

"How do you think he found us?" Billy Bones said.

"I'm not quite sure," Conrad said loudly enough for his counterpart to hear. "But I think we have to take his arrival at our home very seriously. This man isn't just your run-of-the-mill ordinary spy. He appears to be some sort of genius secret agent. I'm afraid we are all in grave danger."

"What should we do?"

Conrad threw his cape over one shoulder. "We must take his surfacing at our residence as a direct threat. He is a wily one, I assure you. For him to sit in our dining hall calmly reading a book and not even glance in our direction takes nerves of steel. The crossbow is out of the question now. This kind of spy is trained to dodge arrows and bullets. We have to break out the heavy artillery. Get me the briefcase."

Alfred ran across the room and pulled the briefcase from the back of the closet. He brought it over to Conrad and opened the case in front of his fearless leader. Conrad placed his hands on the objects inside and felt around for one item in particular. He found it in the far left corner.

"I need a volunteer," he said.

Neither Billy Bones nor Alfred spoke up.

Conrad shook his head. "You both know that I would do this if I could see but I damn well can't. Now one of you needs to show some courage and take a little initiative here."

Billy Bones and Alfred remained quiet, their eyes fixed on the floor.

"Fine," Conrad lost his temper a little. "This is how we'll do it. I'm going to count to three and we'll all say *Not it*. The last person to say *Not it* gets the assignment. Any objections?"

Alfred screamed a vigorous objection but it got caught in his windpipe and never escaped his mouth.

"One, two, three, *Not it!*" Conrad said.

Alfred tried to yell but couldn't make a sound.

Billy Bones had forgotten entirely what they were talking about and was picturing the nurse's soft, round breasts in his mind. He thought perhaps he could barter a better deal and use only $1,500 of his bounty money to see them.

"Bones!" Conrad forgot to fake his English accent. "Yell *Not it!*"

"Not it!" Billy Bones screamed.

Conrad turned to Alfred with a reluctant frown. His accent returned with renewed vigor. "I'm afraid, old friend, that the assignment falls on you."

Irritably, Alfred snatched the object out of Conrad's hand.

Conrad laid out some simple instructions. "You pull the pin out from the top in order to activate it. Then so long as you're holding it, nothing will happen. But as soon as you let it go, you have only six seconds to get away or you risk facing certain death."

Alfred nodded.

He was squeezing it tightly in his right hand when for some inexplicable reason unknown even to him, Billy Bones reached over and pulled out the pin. Conrad heard the click as the pin dislodged and frantically tried to grab it back out of Billy's hand but couldn't see well enough to find it. Meanwhile Alfred closed his eyes and hoped not to die. Six excruciating seconds passed and nothing happened. They were still alive. Both Conrad and Alfred breathed a sigh of relief. Billy Bones stood to the side with a look of general confusion on his face.

"Now go get him, old chap," Conrad said. He ushered Alfred toward the door and shut it behind him.

Alfred headed down the hallway toward the washroom — a live grenade in his hand.

The inside of the lavatory was a palace. The stall Henrik typically used at work was a filthy eggshell white with all manner of graffiti on the walls. Each time Henrik sat down to relieve himself during his break, he would stare directly at a lyric some surprisingly eloquent degenerate had scribbled on the back of the door —

Oh vile feces
Drop swift and whole
Flee this cold, dark cell

Henrik always felt rushed at work.

In contrast, the stall Henrik selected in the retirement home was nearly three quarters the size of his whole apartment. Built specifically for the residents with osteoporosis, it featured several handrails, an emergency button and a full reading section flourishing with books, magazines and a stack of old newspapers. Henrik settled in comfortably and was having quite an agreeable bowel movement when he reached down and selected an old faded newspaper from the bottom of the pile. On the front page was disgraced American senator Larry Craig. Henrik read that the senator had recently been arrested for and pled guilty to the crime of *cottaging*, which, Henrik would learn, was soliciting anonymous gay sexual activity in public bathrooms. Senator Craig was now telling everyone who would listen that he wasn't guilty and that he was a victim of police entrapment. Henrik didn't believe him. But he did read on about the details of *cottaging*. Apparently it involves making a great deal of eye contact in an airport lavatory before committing offenses against God in a stall meant for bodily functions. Sometimes it's initiated by the tapping of one's foot in the stall next to another person trying to complete their bowel function.

Henrik felt quite sorry for the senator's wife, who now had to go to fancy dinners and PTA meetings with everyone staring at her and knowing deep down that her husband was a hypocrite and a pervert. But he didn't feel strongly either way about what the senator did in airport bathrooms.

Mostly, Henrik was concerned that a public restroom was an unhygienic place to have sexual activity of any kind. In fact, when Henrik sat down on this very toilet, his penis had made incidental contact with the seat and he was now worried that he might develop some sort of rash. This fear of getting a rash was starting to affect the quality and duration of his bowel movement when the lavatory door creaked open.

Alfred entered the washroom and was carrying the live grenade with the utmost care. He took twelve dreadfully tentative steps until he reached Henrik's stall.

Henrik sat on his toilet seat and grumbled to himself, knowing it would be much more difficult and embarrassing to finish with someone else in the room. He set the newspaper down and covered his ears with his hands so he wouldn't hear the other gentleman and could pretend he was alone. To Henrik's abject horror, the man peered through the crack in his stall and then entered the booth next to him. This was not good. There were plenty of other stalls he could have selected.

Henrik knew exactly what was going on.

"Hello?" he said.

The man didn't reply. Inside Henrik's brain, alarm bells rang.

Little did Henrik know that on the other side of the divider, Alfred was feverishly trying to get Henrik to identify himself. He hadn't been able to see Henrik through the crack in the stall door and wasn't about to dump a live grenade on someone without at least establishing their identity first. Alfred continued to demand that the man say his name but no sound actually escaped his lips. He attempted to stand up on the toilet and peer into the next stall but his rickety old legs shook terribly and catastrophe almost struck as he nearly dropped the live grenade. Unable to think of anything else, Alfred tapped his foot on the floor to get Henrik's attention.

Henrik's brain nearly exploded in shock. Furiously, he tore off a wad of toilet paper and wiped his bottom as fast as he could.

From the other side, a frustrated Alfred reached underneath the divider and was about to drop the grenade when Henrik snatched it out of his hand. Henrik clenched the grenade tightly, frightened to his core, but not sure what the hell this thing was. He had to assume, from all the empirical evidence at his disposal — the attempted eye contact through the door, the foot tapping and the offering of a peculiar gift — that this metal object was some sort of bizarre device used in sexual gratification.

The moment he released the grenade, Alfred turned and ran from the bathroom as fast as his old legs would take him. The lavatory door opened and shut with a resonant thud. Alone again, Henrik zipped up with one hand and looked at the metal object in the other. Part of him was curious as to what the hell he was supposed to do with this thing. The other part (perhaps fifteen percent of him) was a little wounded that the man left so quickly without further attempts to woo him.

Henrik poked his head out of the bathroom stall to make sure there was no one there. Ever since he saw the tapping foot, he'd felt an urge to flee the retirement home. The window on the far wall was much too high and far too small for him to reach or squeeze through. He would have to make a break for it out the lavatory door. Henrik placed his hand on the door handle, cautiously hoping that there was no horny old man on the other side. He opened the door and peered a single eyeball into the hallway. It was empty save for a little old lady walking by herself toward the women's washroom. Henrik summoned all his courage and stepped into the corridor. He put one foot in front of the other and marched down the hallway.

The elderly woman stopped him.

"Are you going to finish reading to us?" she said.

"No," Henrik said.

"Well, did you bring us anything from the outside? Some news perhaps?" She leaned in close and lowered her voice. "They don't like us to leave, you know. The reaper is always right around the corner."

Henrik paused, considered saying something nice and then did the exact opposite.

"I brought you this present," Henrik said as he handed her the live grenade. He snickered a little to himself, wondering if the old lady would know what to do with the strange sex object.

The old woman took the grenade in her hands. Her heart jumped into her throat when she realized what it was. Only she couldn't hand it back to Henrik. He was already circling the end of the hallway. She dropped the grenade in a panic.

Henrik stormed toward the front doors, past the stage area where a few of the more senile residents were still waiting for him to finish his performance. As he passed the receptionist, she asked him whether he was still going to read to the old folks. Henrik told her that this place was full of *cottaging* perverts and thank you but no, he wasn't going to read *Moby Dick* to a bunch of perverts. She tried to say something else but Henrik put his hands up to his ears and mumbled loudly so he couldn't hear.

 sixteen

It was a good thing he had his hands over his ears.

They mostly muffled the sound of an old woman exploding in the hallway behind him.

Henrik left the retirement home and stepped straight into a taxicab. He paid no heed to the thunderous explosion behind him. For all he knew, a minor earthquake might have shaken the ground or perhaps three morbidly obese pensioners had fallen out of their lawn chairs at the exact same time. Henrik didn't care. He wanted to get out of there as fast as he could. He told the driver to take him to the nearest hospital. The driver sped off down the street and Henrik finally put some distance between himself and those *cottaging* old people.

He couldn't relax, however. Henrik now felt there was something really wrong with his penis. It had touched the toilet seat back in the bathroom and while the actual contact was quite brief and were Henrik to be forced to describe the convergence of skin and plastic, he most likely would have used the phrase *a slight grazing*, he nonetheless was growing more and more worried with each passing second. He could still feel where his penis had touched the seat. This wasn't normal. Henrik could not typically feel the presence of his penis. He tried feeling the presence of his shins and his elbows without actually touching them in order to gauge whether or not he was going crazy. Much to his dismay, he could feel neither his shins nor his elbows. Nor could he sense anything in the toes he had just clipped that afternoon. From the evidence at hand — the strange sensation on his penis and the lack of sensation on the rest of his body — Henrik self-diagnosed that he'd received some manner of venereal disease from the toilet seat.

He entered the hospital emergency room and braced himself for the carnage. The last time Henrik visited the ER, he encountered dozens of people crowded into the waiting room, each and every one of them sneezing or coughing, wheezing or oozing, displaying visible wounds or hunched over in some manner of terrible pain. It was a scene very much like the congested employment office, only with the walking wounded huddled in corners, with pestilence and disease lingering in the air. Henrik was surprised — shocked, rather — to see just three patients in the emergency room waiting area, a young woman with her daughter and a middle-aged lady sitting across from them. He walked up to the front desk where a nurse was wearing a set of purple hospital pajamas.

"I'd like to see a doctor, please."

"What does this pertain to?"

"Pardon me?" Henrik said.

"What's the nature of your illness?"

"I'd really rather speak to the doctor," he said.

The nurse in the purple pajamas told Henrik it would take up to forty-five minutes and that he should have a seat in the waiting room. Henrik walked over and sat down among the others. Whether it was to suppress his rapidly increasing anxiety or just to break the empty silence in the room, Henrik felt an urge to talk to his fellow patients.

"What are you in for?" he said to the middle-aged woman.

She looked up from her Sudoku. "Gallstones mainly."

Henrik nodded.

"Also, there's this itch I have on my elbow." She set her puzzle book on her lap and pulled her sleeve up to reveal the raw, red area she'd been scratching. "Also," she said quietly, "it might be my diet, but lately my digestive tract has been a disaster. It's like a fireworks display that you never see coming. There's been a few close calls recently. A couple of races to the finish line." She proceeded to tell Henrik a story about a disastrous attempt to find a washroom at a local gardening store.

Henrik stood up as the woman was untying her shoe to show him a gangrenous nail and sat down beside the little girl in the adjacent row. Five minutes passed in silence. Henrik's sense of urgency was still escalating exponentially by the minute when he noticed something out of the corner of his eye. This little girl, no more than five years old and forty pounds soaking wet, had some sort of pox on her skin. A series of boils had manifested on her cheeks, arms and hands. The smaller inflammations were relegated to her face while the larger ones had assembled along her forearms. Henrik didn't know what it was — measles, smallpox, the Egyptian plague — but it was starting to scare the hell out of him.

Just then an agonized scream sounded. Henrik peered down the hallway to see a man in a Dunkin' Donuts uniform lying in a hospital bed with an arrow sticking out of his chest. The man kept yelling. From what Henrik could discern, the Dunkin' Donuts employee had been waiting for hours for a specialist to remove the arrow and was incensed that others were receiving attention while he had yet to meet with the specialist.

A female doctor told him to be quiet, shut a curtain around him and walked over to the waiting room. She looked down at her clipboard.

"Mr. Nordmark? Please come with me."

Henrik stood up and followed the doctor. She placed him on a bed next to the angry man.

"I'm Dr. Simmers," she said. "Now what seems to be the problem today?"

Henrik wasn't sure quite where to start. He took a deep breath and informed her that (A) he was really impressed with the speed at which the medical system in this country operated and (B) he had just received a venereal disease from a toilet in a retirement home. By the slight but discernable way the doctor rolled her eyes, Henrik suspected she thought he was making up the sensation in order to show her his genitals. She must have thought he was some kind of pervert. Henrik said, "If you want to meet a pervert, go back to the old folks' home. That's where all the perverts are."

The doctor gave him a stunned look.

Perhaps, Henrik thought, I misread her eye roll.

The doctor hesitated, like she was deciding whether or not to send Henrik on his way, then gave him a light blue hospital gown and told him to get undressed. She closed the curtain on the way out. Henrik slipped out of his uniform and into the hospital gown. It barely fit around his stomach girth and he had to hold it closed at the back to avoid revealing his buttocks.

While the doctor was gone, the injured man in the next section continued to yell. He even threatened to sue. A second patient who had intentionally digested a fork and a spoon in a desperate bid for attention was sitting two beds over. She yelled that she'd had enough of the Dunkin' Donuts employee's whining and that he only wanted to sue because he made minimum wage and he wanted to get rich without actually having to work for the money.

Finally the female doctor came back. She told them both to keep it down or she'd call security, then closed the curtain around Henrik, put on a pair of plastic gloves and took a look at his penis. After a lightning-fast assessment, she told him there was absolutely no rash to be seen.

"Is there anything else?" she said.

Henrik was about to shake his head no, but instead gave his current condition a great deal of thought. Perhaps there was something else wrong with him. Perhaps there'd always been something terribly wrong with his body but he'd grown so accustomed to the feeling of being gravely ill that he didn't even realize he was sick. Henrik asked the doctor to perform a full physical examination. She told him she didn't have time for that and he'd have to make an appointment with his general practitioner. The way she rolled her eyes when she answered told Henrik that she still suspected him of egregious perversity.

She was about to leave so Henrik told her lately he'd been feeling an overwhelming compulsion to wash his hands at least seventeen times a day.

"There's nothing wrong with that," she said. "In fact, you should wash your hands every possible chance you get. Wash them twenty or thirty times a day."

"Really?" he said. "Is that healthy?"

"Of course it is. Clean hands are very healthy."

"But wouldn't a lifetime of compulsive hand-washing

affect my mental health?"

The doctor shrugged her shoulders.

"Is there anything else?"

She was about to leave again when Henrik felt himself on the verge of panic. *There must be something wrong with me*, he thought. *There must be some vile affliction that I have that people will want to hear about and discuss.* He thought of the greatest first baseman of all time, Lou Gehrig, and what a lucky bastard he'd been to have a disease named after him. Henrik started complaining of random ailments in his ankles, nostrils and buttocks in a desperate search for something, anything to make the doctor stay. He was enjoying the attention. And, more importantly, if he strained his eyes hard enough, he could almost see down her blouse.

The doctor seemed irritated. She looked Henrik straight in the eye and said that what he had was a simple case of hypochondria. She accused him of making up illnesses and told him it was a really common thing to do.

"Common?" Henrik said.

"Yes," she said, trying to make him feel better but in fact making him feel infinitely worse. "It's a very typical condition. Many people have it. Ordinary people without any real afflictions believe they must have something wrong with them, and some people actually develop psychosomatic symptoms that mimic the condition they believe they have. But don't worry," she said, "You'll be just fine. You're not going to die."

Henrik listened as she spoke but didn't hear anything about not dying or not worrying. The only words he heard were common and typical and ordinary.

In the distance, the emergency room doors burst open

and an elderly woman was wheeled into the hospital on a gurney. She'd lost both her arms and a great deal of her torso in an explosion. One of the orderlies referred to her as a goner, which caused her grandson, who was trailing behind the gurney, to let out a grief-stricken cry. Henrik looked through the curtain and recognized him as the young man who struggled with the fifteenth-floor security guards as he was escorted from his office building. It appeared the young man's day had gotten much worse as he now had a partially decapitated grandmother to deal with. Henrik's doctor, the grandson and the blown-up grandmother rounded the corner into another room and suddenly it fell very quiet.

Henrik reflected on the doctor's words. Eventually he came to the realization that there was nothing at all wrong with his penis or the rest of him. He stripped out of his hospital gown and was putting on his security guard uniform when a woman poked her head in. It was Bonnie, the woman Henrik bumped into in the marketplace, inadvertently making her the winner of four million dollars. Henrik didn't recognize her at all but she immediately recognized him.

Bonnie tried to play it cool. If this bald man found out about the switched tickets, he might alert the lottery officials and she could very well lose her still-unclaimed grand prize.

"Have you seen a man with an arrow wound?" she said. "He's probably wearing a Dunkin' Donuts uniform."

"I'm right here," Clyde said from the other side of the sheet.

Henrik pointed to his right.

Bonnie smiled and entered the next partition. Her husband Clyde was lying on the bed in obvious pain. Bonnie walked over and tried to kiss him. Clyde rebuked her affections and turned his head the other way.

"What's wrong?" she said.

"What's wrong? I got shot in the chest with an arrow four hours ago and you've finally just shown up at the hospital now. *That's* what's wrong."

"I was working," Bonnie said.

Her irritability did not sit well with Clyde. He himself was quite irate.

"You still should have come as soon as you heard."

"I couldn't leave my job," she said. "There was no one to cover for me and the doctor told me on the phone that you weren't going to die. I don't know what you're so angry about."

"Screw your job!"

Bonnie stepped forward and slapped her husband across the face. It was the first time she'd ever hit him.

"I don't know why you can't support my work," she said. "My parents support me. They come to my work at least once a week. Even our priest joined them a few times. You're the only one who has anything bad to say about my job."

Clyde could smell cigarettes on Bonnie's skin and a hint of vodka on her breath. He grew even angrier.

"Why did you have to tell the guy next to me that I work at Dunkin' Donuts?"

"Because you do work at Dunkin' Donuts, you jackass! You shouldn't be ashamed of your job."

"You only tell people I work at Dunkin' Donuts because you want them to know I earn minimum wage and I can't support us."

"That's not it at all," she said. "I asked that guy if he'd seen a man wearing a Dunkin' Donuts uniform because *you're wearing a fucking Dunkin' Donuts uniform.* If you were wearing a suit, I would have asked him if he saw a man in a suit."

"But I'm not wearing a suit!"

"No," Bonnie rolled her tongue along the inside of her cheek. "You're not wearing a suit, are you?"

Henrik had fully pulled on his clothes and was listening through the curtain, hearing the argument escalate. These two had grown so incensed that their voices rose with every word.

"I know you screwed that little skank from Orange Julius," she said.

"I told you — I didn't screw her," Clyde lied.

"I could cheat on you too," she said.

Clyde laughed a little. "Listen, we both know that's not going to happen. Look at you. Look at what you do for a living. You're a stripper! You take off your clothes for money."

"How dare you?" Bonnie's voice rose in volume and fury. "I'm a dancer! And I've worked damn hard to get to where I'm at in life. Three years ago, where was I? Working the Tuesday afternoon lunch crowd and subbing at Bart's House of Class on C-Section Sundays. Now I'm one of the top girls. People love what I do. Men want me."

Clyde shook his head. "No one else wants you. I'm all you've got, babe. I'm all you'll ever have."

Bonnie stomped her foot furiously on the ground. She looked around for something to hit Clyde with and made accidental eye contact with Henrik as he walked by Clyde's curtain and glanced in. Bonnie stormed over and flung the curtain open. She grabbed Henrik's surprised face in her hands and planted a big, sloppy wet kiss on his mouth. Four and a half long seconds passed before Bonnie released Henrik and tossed him back toward the other bed.

She turned to Clyde and gave him a look of wretched loathing. Bonnie had hidden her hatred for too long. Her face morphed into a hideous scowl.

Alarm bells sounded in Clyde's head. He looked down at the arrow still stuck in his chest. "You did this to me, didn't you?"

"Don't be preposterous!"

"Preposterous, eh?" Clyde said. "That's a pretty big word for someone who didn't even finish ninth grade."

A wild glare formed in Bonnie's eyes. She lunged at Clyde and grabbed hold of the arrow. Bonnie started twisting it in circles. Clyde let out a tormented scream and tried to stop her.

"I've been trying to kill you for months!"

"I'll kill you!"

"No, *I'll* kill *you!*"

Finally a set of orderlies, until now busy with the blown-up grandmother, came over to see what all the ruckus was about.

Henrik had fallen to the ground when Bonnie pushed him away. He scrambled to his feet and watched Bonnie and Clyde battle it out. When the orderlies arrived, they pulled a kicking and screaming Bonnie off her husband while Henrik stumbled out of the emergency room and into the street.

Henrik held his fingers up to his lips. No woman had ever kissed him before. It was the most joyous sensation he'd ever experienced. Past the taste of vodka and beyond the odor of old cigarettes, there was something euphoric about that strange woman's tongue swirling around his mouth. Like licking a hundred miniature caramelized apples. Henrik felt amazing. A miracle was embedded in that kiss. He longed to feel it again. And he wasn't the least bit discouraged by the ugly display of marital relations he saw back in the hospital. Henrik had finally decided how he would become special and unique.

He would find someone to love him and to kiss him.

He would find himself a girlfriend.

seventeen

Of course, Henrik had absolutely no idea of how to go about getting a girlfriend. He went home and got a good night's sleep, confident that his subconscious would determine the best way to make a woman fall in love with him. When Henrik woke up the next morning, he scurried over to the table where he had a pen and piece of paper waiting to record whatever bright ideas his subconscious mind had come up with. Unfortunately there were none. He'd awoken to a strange dream about the season of *The Dukes of Hazzard* in which they'd inconceivably changed their lead actors over a merchandise profit-sharing dispute. He couldn't get the picture of the General Lee jumping a row of cars out of his head and set the paper down, greatly agitated that his subconscious hadn't been more supportive or accommodating.

After a torturous hour spent — literally — staring at the wall, Henrik realized he would never find a girlfriend on his own. He decided it was best to seek out expert knowledge on the subject of human mating. Henrik forwent the Costco-sized bookstore with its nosy employees and magazines wrapped in cellophane and ambled over to the local bookshop, where he headed straight to the sexuality section and bought half a dozen books on relationships, erotica and the Kama Sutra. The attractive woman behind the counter gave him an apprehensive look when he approached the desk. Henrik found her quite striking and briefly considered starting his foray into the dating scene by asking her to share a cup of coffee with him. But then he remembered that he had yet to read all of these informative books and that it was better to come into such a situation armed with knowledge rather than ignorance.

"Are these the best books on human relations?" he said.

The woman hesitated before answering. "I think they are."

"Thank you."

Henrik made a mental note to one day return to this bookstore and perform the Kama Sutra on the attractive cashier.

He headed straight home and flipped through the books. Henrik started with the picture-laden volumes that promised to teach him various sexual techniques. The more he looked at pictures of bondage, Nyotaimori (sexual food play) and Bukkakes (a really mean thing to do), the more he realized he was jumping too far ahead by learning what to do sexually to a woman without first learning how to trick her into his bed.

He'd anticipated the relationship books would be more instructional in nature but they proved equally confusing. Some of them even contradicted what the others said. One of the books (written by a woman) told Henrik that men fundamentally don't understand sexual intercourse and that there must be a long drawn-out ending and at minimum twenty minutes of cuddling in order for it to be enjoyable for both participants. A second book (written by a man) told him that this was all hogwash and that when men are done, they're done. Henrik didn't know what to believe. He picked up another book and learned that men are from Mars and women are from Venus but the book said nothing about the origin planet of homosexuals. The general inference was that they didn't exist at all. This confused Henrik to no end. He was quite sure that there were at minimum thirty homosexuals on Earth because over the course of his lifetime, Henrik had witnessed fifteen incidents of same-sex kissing, and counting up the participants on both hands, he came to a total of thirty. Thirty-one if you count that *cottaging* bastard Senator Larry Craig.

He threw the relationship books aside. They were obviously lying to him. Henrik grew suddenly angry with that attractive cashier in the bookstore. She had lied to him when she said these were the best books he could buy. Henrik now hated her beyond all reason. He most certainly *would not* return and perform the Kama Sutra on her.

Henrik languished in his chair. He planned to spend the entire day cursing his misfortune — and perhaps if he had time, performing some extensive soul-searching — when suddenly a sensation akin to a lightning bolt struck the base of his skull. From there it spread outward; tortoise-like at first, it gained momentum as it sailed through his brain, bashing aside neurons and careening off the hypothalamus before the sensation formed a single thought so akin to a great idea, Henrik didn't know what hit him. He ran over to the kitchen and opened the cupboard above the refrigerator. Henrik slammed a copy of the Yellow Pages on the counter and flipped sections back and forth like a madman until he found the page he was looking for. There in large black letters was the word MATCHMAKER. Henrik grabbed his phone and dialed the number at the top of the page.

One hour later Henrik was sitting in the matchmaker's office across town. He'd put on his best suit before he left the apartment and, hell-bent as he was on making a good impression, had cleaned behind his ears, brushed his teeth and even rinsed his mouth twice with blue mouthwash he'd found in an old dusty bottle under his bathroom sink.

The receptionist walked him into an office and Henrik sat down across from the matchmaker. She introduced herself as Susan. Susan had wide eyes spaced far apart on her head, big breasts and a tight brown leather jacket. She looked to be about fifty-five years old, a good four years older than the arbitrary twenty-seven– through fifty-one–year age range Henrik had randomly decided upon for a prospective mate. Susan smiled warmly.

Henrik immediately felt at ease in her presence. He crossed his legs and leaned back in his seat a little.

"Some advice?" Susan said. "You should always sit up straight in front of a lady. Especially in a dating situation. Sitting up straight indicates you are a man of power. A man of action. Slouching gives your entire body an aura of being flaccid. Women don't like men who are flaccid."

Henrik sat up straight and smiled bravely at the woman.

"Also, never cross your legs so tightly. It gives others the impression you have a small penis. Women frown greatly upon men with small penises."

Henrik uncrossed his legs and made a mental note to never ever cross them again.

"Now," Susan said. "How may I help you today?"

"I would like to find a girlfriend."

"Have you dated before?"

"No. This would be my first time."

"Well then, let's start by me asking a few questions. First, how old are you?"

"Forty-two."

"How much money do you make?"

Henrik hesitated.

"Is it less than thirty thousand, less than sixty thousand or less than ninety thousand?"

"The first one."

The matchmaker made a sour face.

"Do you live alone with your mother?" she said.

"No."

"How long did you live alone with your mother before you moved out?"

"I've never lived alone with my mother," Henrik said.

"Never?"

"Never," Henrik said. "And I fail to see how whether or not I ever lived alone with my mother should affect my ability to find a girlfriend."

"Well, you're forty-two years old and you say this is your first time dating?"

"Yes."

The matchmaker gathered her eyebrows and turned her attention to the open folder on her desk. She proceeded to write down extensive notes on a piece of yellow paper, with intricate details and observations on their current conversation. Some of the notes were in full sentences, others in point form and together they took up the entire side of the page and a small portion at the top of the other side. The matchmaker wrote without looking up, intermittently exhaling long breaths out through her nose, before she finally turned her attention back to Henrik again.

"Have you ever heard of Sigmund Freud?"

"I'm familiar with his early work." Henrik lied wholeheartedly and without conscience.

"Really?" Susan said. "Which portions of his early work?"

"The early, early portions."

"Are you familiar with his theory of the Oedipus complex?"

"No," Henrik said. "That must have been part of his later work."

"Freud believed that each son secretly desires to marry his mother and kill his father."

"What does this have to do with me?" he said.

"You're forty-two years old and you've never been on a date. Based on these facts alone, I suspect you're a textbook case of Oedipal desire."

"But my mother is a thick-wristed German woman who weighs nearly three hundred pounds."

"All the same," the matchmaker said.

"And my father is dead."

"I rest my case."

Henrik was largely offended. He was paying one hundred dollars for this appointment and had spent the entirety of it being accused of acts he'd never considered — not even once — in his entire life. Henrik would have lashed out verbally had he not been so busy marveling at how unique a person must be to have constant thoughts of incest and patricide running through his head. Now, that was inimitable distinctiveness if Henrik ever heard of it.

Susan pushed her leather jacket up to her elbows and cracked her knuckles. "What type of woman are you looking for?"

"I'm not sure. I'm in no position to be picky."

"But you must have a type in mind. Someone athletic perhaps?"

"I don't want to be encouraged to do calisthenics," Henrik said.

"Perhaps you're looking for someone feisty?"

"What does that mean?"

"You know, abrasive and bossy. The kind of woman who picks out your shirts for you and enjoys sending back soup at a restaurant."

Henrik shifted in his seat. "I don't think I want someone that feisty."

"How about someone more traditional? The kind of woman who likes you to hold the door open for her?"

"That sounds terrific," Henrik said.

"Not so fast. The traditional woman will also expect you to pay for her whenever you go to dinner. And she's likely to make you wait until marriage before you have sex."

"Oh."

This sounded absolutely terrible to Henrik. Conceivably, he wouldn't mind waiting until marriage to have sexual intercourse. In fact, a traditional woman might even marry him without ever learning about his significant lack of skills in the bedroom. But he loathed the idea that he would have to pay double for dinner and movies every time they went out. And what would his well-paid, traditional girlfriend be doing this whole while? No doubt investing her money in 401ks and real estate properties, stocks and bonds. Her mattress would be stuffed with dollar bills and her piggy bank overflowing with change while Henrik ate at soup kitchens and purchased his clothing from the Salvation Army.

And when she inevitably left him for another man, the traditional woman would go on her way carrying a thick investment portfolio under her arm while Henrik was left poor, heartbroken and sexually frustrated to the point where he didn't know whether to cry or scream. No, this didn't sound like a good idea at all.

"Perhaps a traditional woman isn't right for me either," Henrik said.

"Okay," Susan said. "Just for a minute, let's forget about what type of woman you're looking for. What I try to do is match people on the basis of several factors of compatibility. Age, religion, sexual preference, relative vigor of libido — everything down to which side of the bed you sleep on. But let's face it. The most significant factor is looks. People have to be within the same range on a scale of attractiveness in order for a relationship to work.

"For example, if I have a male client who is an eight out of ten — solid jaw, slim and with all his original teeth — it's only wise for me to set him up with someone close to his level of attractiveness. So my client who's an eight can date someone as low as a six-point-five, like the kind of woman you see on the escalator at the mall. Or, should he be so lucky, as high as a nine-point-five."

"Who would be a nine-point-five?"

"Imagine Jennifer Aniston in season one of *Friends*."

"Then who would be a seven?"

"Jennifer Aniston in season six of *Friends*."

"Oh."

"From my experience, if two clients aren't within the same range on the scale, it never works out."

Susan leaned forward.

"So, let me ask you honestly: how would you rate yourself?"

Henrik paused to think. He started to have another flashback to the image of himself in the mismatched secondhand clothes dancing alone in front of the mirror. He pushed the image back in his mind until it lurked in the cobwebs with theme songs to movies from the '70s and an innocuous episode of the short-lived Harlem Globetrotters cartoon.

"I suppose if I'm answering honestly, I'd say I'm about a three out of ten."

"Thank you." Susan turned away from Henrik and logged onto a computer at the side of her desk. The matchmaker clicked around with the mouse and typed on her keyboard for several minutes in silence, the whole while breathing hard through her nose. Henrik could tell by the various picture profiles brought up on the screen and the amount of clicking that she was performing an exhaustive search through her database of female clients.

Finally Susan turned back from her computer.

"Nothing."

"Nothing?"

Susan shook her head.

"If you don't have any threes," Henrik said, "perhaps you have someone as low as a one-point-five. I'm willing to start at the bottom and work my way up."

"Sorry. The lowest I have is a five-point-five out of ten."

"Maybe I was being a little too modest," he said. "Perhaps I'm closer to a five."

Susan stared at him. Henrik looked back at her with a set of puppy-dog eyes but Susan's expression didn't change.

"If I were you, Mr. Nordmark," she said quietly, "I'd stick with your original assessment."

Henrik felt a pang of desperation in his chest.

"Perhaps there's some way for me to make up the difference

of that point; you know, to go from a three to a four."

Susan pulled a piece of cinnamon gum out of her purse and chewed loudly while she spoke. "Are you in line for a windfall inheritance?"

"No."

"Do you drive a nice car?"

"I take the bus."

Susan sighed. "Then I won't be able to help you."

Henrik shuffled anxiously in his seat. "So you're telling me there's not one woman in your files who would be a good match for me?"

The matchmaker paused.

"Mr. Nordmark, have you ever seen a zombie movie?"

"Maybe once on television."

"Good, then you'll know what I'm talking about. I'm not a fan of horror movies but my son from my second marriage dragged me to one last week. Essentially the plot involved the last few humans on Earth running away from flesh-eating monsters. It was actually pretty entertaining. But do you know what struck me as the most interesting part of the entire movie? That there are two types of people in this world. There are capable, swift, fast-minded people who can make quick decisions and escape a stampeding horde of the undead. Then there are people like you, Mr. Nordmark. Zombie food. People who, through *direct* fault of their own, wouldn't even make it twenty paces before tripping over their own two feet and causing the entire party of fleeing humans to be captured and eaten."

"I don't follow what you're saying," Henrik said.

Susan exhaled through her nose again.

"I'll admit I'm basing this all on first impressions, but I have a responsibility to my clients. We're more of a boutique agency here. And I'm like a chef in a fancy restaurant. I wouldn't serve something to one of my customers unless I wanted to eat it myself. As a matchmaker, I can't recommend you to one of my clients unless I see one redeemable characteristic that makes my wheels turn."

Susan lowered her voice.

"Besides, Mr. Nordmark, if I did set you up with a woman and by the grace of God you somehow miraculously convinced her to enter your bedroom, would you even know what to do with her?"

Henrik gave the woman a look of stunned disbelief. Seven point eight seconds passed, with the two of them, matchmaker and client, staring in each other's direction but not directly at one another, before Henrik said, "Can I have my hundred dollars back?"

Susan rolled down the sleeves on her tight leather coat and turned off her computer screen. She stared at the desk for a moment and then looked up. "No."

Henrik left the matchmaker's office with a dark cloud of despair hanging over his head. He walked the streets until he reached a small park where he sat down alone on a bench and stared at the motionless swing set. His mind played the matchmaker's words over again in his head — if he did convince a woman to sleep with him, would he even know what the hell to do with her? Truthfully, no. Aside from the basic notion of which body part goes where, he had absolutely no idea. Henrik had no prospects, no money, no vehicle and no fornication skills.

"I must apply logic to this situation," he said. He decided to look at the complex problem of human mating with objective reason. If Henrik wanted to learn how to sew, he would pay for sewing lessons. And if he wanted to learn how to skate, he would pay for skating lessons. If he wanted to learn how to seduce a woman, logic dictated that he first take seduction lessons.

Henrik stood up on the park bench and felt the cool breeze against his face. The wind picked up and ruffled the collar of his jacket. A smile curled at the corners of Henrik's mouth. He hopped off the bench and marched toward the bus stop with a look of determination on his face.

Henrik was going to find himself a prostitute.

eighteen

Bonnie's hand shook as she inserted her key into the apartment door. Her eyes darted down the hall. Clyde was nowhere to be seen. She turned the key, heard the tiny click of metal inside the lock and edged the door open. "Hello?" Bonnie said. "Hello?" she called again, louder this time. Bonnie opened the door all the way. With one final glance behind her, she slipped inside the apartment and closed the door. Bonnie stood absolutely still.

At the hospital yesterday, her fight with her husband had spilled out onto the street and Clyde — with the arrow still protruding from his chest — took off before the police could catch him. Bonnie also sneaked away before being arrested, intent on going into seclusion. But first she needed to protect herself. Bonnie scurried over to the kitchen, her high heels clicking on the hardwood floors, and rummaged through the cupboards. There, past the baking supplies and behind a spice rack full of outdated herbs, Bonnie found what she was looking for. She pulled out a three-year-old box of Count Chocula cereal and reached inside. Bonnie's hand grasped the gun. The metal felt cold against her skin. She pulled the tiny pistol out and brushed off the flakes of cereal dust.

"I should have used this years ago," Bonnie said. She cocked the gun and pointed it toward the door.

The simple truth was that Bonnie would have shot Clyde

long ago if she wasn't so afraid of prison. It's one thing to hurl your husband down an empty elevator shaft. There's plausible deniability in a fall from a great height. The whole event reeks of an accident. It's another thing entirely to pull the trigger and pretend you didn't do it. What with forensic evidence these days and the proliferation of three or four different *CSI* shows on television, everyone was an expert now. Even Bonnie, who dropped out of high school to party with frat boys and work odd jobs at the mini-mall, knew about blood spatter analysis and gun powder residue. Had her earlier attempts at poisoning Clyde's coffee been successful, she could have explained his death as a suicide. But if she shot her husband dead in cold blood, it was likely she would spend the rest of her life behind bars.

Now she might have no choice.

Bonnie tucked the gun under her belt and hurried into the bedroom. In a frenzy, she packed a bag of her things, grabbed her jacket and fished some money out of the desk drawer before running toward the front door. As she opened the door, she knocked over the umbrella holder. The ceramic unicorn fell to the ground with a clank and cracked right down the center. Bonnie stared at her precious unicorn, the one she'd braved the hideous stench and oily garbage bags to retrieve from the refuse bin downstairs. Everything around her was crumbling to dust. She paused, took a deep breath and stepped out into the hallway.

And then she stopped.

There was Clyde, that fiend, the man who had vowed to kill her yesterday, now less than forty feet down the hall. He had just stepped off the elevator, the arrow still lodged in his chest. Bonnie shut the door before Clyde could see her and stood with her back against the wall. A chill ran down her spine; sweat formed a clammy paste on her lower back. In one hand, Bonnie held her bag full of clothes, in the other — the cold metal of the gun. Clyde's lumbering footsteps were drawing nearer with every passing moment. Bonnie glanced at the window. Their apartment was fourteen floors up and there was no fire escape: there wasn't even a ledge outside the window on which she could shimmy and hide.

The footsteps were getting closer, louder.

Bonnie closed her eyes and pictured the aftermath of a grisly murder in which she'd shot Clyde five times in the chest and was sentenced to life in prison; a life of gray prison gruel and showering with tattooed women who were built like trucks. The wrists of her orange jumpsuit would ride up on her arms. The prison guards would rule by intimidation and make her fight other convicted murderers in bizarre cage matches while they stood by the side taking bets and filming the whole thing for release on the hardcore Vietnamese version of YouTube.

No, she couldn't do this. Not now.

She was flirting with the idea of climbing out the window and dangling from the precipice by her fingertips when she heard Clyde's keys jingle on the other side of the door. Bonnie gasped. She stepped away from the wall and the sound of her heels on the hardwood floor, conspicuous before Clyde arrived, now echoed in her ears like miniature sonic booms.

Bonnie took off her shoes and shuffled barefoot across the floor in a desperate search for someplace to hide.

Clyde slammed the door behind him and heaved a painful breath. "Bonnie!" His eyes cast left and then right. "Bonnie!" The apartment lay absolutely still. Clyde staggered over to the kitchen and reached inside the cupboard. He was famished. He pulled out two Fruit Roll-Ups, one orange, the other raspberry, and bit into both at the same time. Clyde gnawed away on them with his back teeth. Sticky sweet, the blend of sugars was like an orgy in his mouth.

Last night, Clyde had gone into hiding. It was only now at 10:30 in the morning that he realized he had to act. The police had chased him out of the hospital and Clyde managed to slip undetected behind a row of ambulances. Still unable to remove the arrow from his chest, he'd taken a taxi — the look on the cab driver's face was one of fearful apprehension — back to the mall, retrieved his Honda Civic and spent the night in his car. As the hours went by, the blood loss caused a faint dizziness to swirl in his head. The tips of his fingers had gone white and two of them felt slightly numb. He had to act now, to kill his wife Bonnie. Before it was too late.

Clyde was standing in the kitchen, one arm propped up on the counter, trying to imagine where Bonnie might be hiding out, when he noticed the empty box of Count Chocula on the counter. He picked it up and dashed the remnants of cereal dust into the sink. Clyde gazed around the living room and back into the hallway. His eyes shifted, suddenly alert. The ceramic unicorn, Bonnie's prized umbrella holder, was lying on its side on the floor, a large crack down the middle.

Clyde spat the Fruit Roll-Ups into the sink.

"Bonnie?" His hands formed tight fists. "Bonnie, where are you?" He crept into the living room and searched with his eyes. "Sweetheart, I forgive you. Come on out and give your husband a kiss." Clyde looked behind the television. He searched every corner, nook and cranny of their living room before heading into the bedroom. With superhuman effort, he bent down to look under the bed. Clyde grabbed the quilt in his hand and pulled it back.

There was no one there.

The bedroom was empty.

With pain in his every step, Clyde hobbled into the bathroom. The light was on. And the shower curtain was closed. *There she is*, he thought. Clyde picked up the hairdryer from the counter and raised it over his head. He took two steps forward and grabbed the shower curtain in his hand. In one sudden motion, Clyde tore the shower curtain open. He swung wildly with the hairdryer.

As Clyde's arm lurched forward, he lost his balance and fell over. The hairdryer ricocheted off the shower tiles and conked Clyde square in the forehead. He toppled over into the bathtub and landed straight on the arrow sticking out of his chest. A fireworks display of red hot pain exploded into every extremity in his body. He screamed out loud and then lay there, limbs twitching, emitting a slight moan, face-planted in the tiles. Thirty seconds passed before he turned his torso awkwardly onto its side and climbed out of the tub. Clyde looked in the mirror. His shirt was covered in blood. The arrow jetted two feet out in the air, stuck in his chest like it was set in concrete. And now he had a budding bruise on his forehead to complete the look of disrepair.

Clyde fumed and grunted. He walked over to the toilet, lifted the cover off the back and flipped it upside down on the counter. There, duct-taped to the underbelly of the toilet lid, was the gun he'd purchased two weeks ago. He tore off the tape and picked up the weapon in his hand.

In the distance, Clyde heard a siren. It sounded like a fire truck, but he wasn't sure. Clyde couldn't take the chance. He took one final look in the mirror and fled the bathroom. Clyde hobbled through the living room and slammed the apartment door.

He left behind a fear-soaked Bonnie, hiding behind the bathroom door and gasping for air — with a loaded nine-millimeter pistol in her sweat-covered hand.

nineteen

Henrik stepped off the bus downtown and immediately began searching up and down the street. Perhaps it had something to do with the fact that it wasn't yet four o'clock in the afternoon and the sun was still in the sky, but finding a prostitute proved much more difficult than he had imagined. And even if he were to spot a streetwalker, Henrik wasn't entirely sure how he would go about approaching her. He still had his rudimentary social graces and wouldn't dare walk up to a random woman and ask her if she was soliciting sex in the street. What if the woman he approached wasn't a prostitute at all but rather just a regular tax-paying citizen who had the misfortune of leaving the house scantily clad on the day Henrik went looking for sex? That would be awkward and embarrassing and Henrik was not about to actively seek awkward, embarrassing situations.

Henrik walked about in a daze for an hour before fate intervened.

Across the street a beautiful young woman was posting a sign on a lamppost that read "25 Dates." *What luck!* Henrik exclaimed. He crossed the street and approached the beautiful woman.

"How much is it for one of your twenty-five dates?" he said.

The woman smiled.

"Have you ever been speed dating before?" she said.

Henrik had never heard the term "speed dating." He decided it must be some sort of code the streetwalkers use to avoid getting arrested.

"I've never been on any sort of date before," he said.

"Well, it's about time you threw your hat into the ring," the woman said.

"How much is it?"

"Forty dollars," she said.

"For all twenty-five dates?"

"Yes."

"Are the dates all with you?" he said.

"No." She giggled.

"So it's forty dollars for twenty-five different dates with twenty-five different women?"

"Yes."

Henrik pulled his money out of his wallet so fast he nearly gave himself a heart attack.

The speed dating woman laughed. "You pay when you arrive at the event," she said. She handed him a card with an address on it and told him to be there that evening at 9 p.m. sharp. Henrik took the card and ambled happily down the street. He was going to have sex with twenty-five different women in one night. He'd never heard of anyone doing that before, not even rock god Ronnie James Dio. Were he able to accomplish such a feat, he would not only make up for a life-time of involuntary chastity, but he would also be revered by his fellow man. Henrik's excitement grew. Tonight his dream would come true. He was finally going to be unique.

twenty

Abraham Arnold parted his blinds and gazed outside. The fire trucks and ambulances, police cars and lookie-loos assembled around the retirement home gates had mostly dispersed. But the news vans and reporters remained. It was almost 6 p.m., the day after the terrible explosion at the retirement home. Abraham brought his hand to his forehead. He'd done everything in his power last night to keep this quiet. A lockdown was declared. The central phone line was disconnected and orderlies were instructed to intimidate any senior who even looked like they might have loose lips. Abraham had almost succeeded. Had it not been for two tech-savvy grandmas in the south wing texting their family on cell phones, this might all have been swept under the rug. Now Abraham stood in his office picturing the content of tonight's evening news. The explosion and the partially decapitated grandmother were bound to be the lead story. Abraham knew reporters, he knew how their minds worked. Despite his quick-witted insistence that Roland's grandmother had been suicidal for months — suicidal and senile, a piteous combination . . . heart-wrenching really — Abraham knew the reporters would turn this into something salacious. They would have a field day with the headlines.

Catastrophe at Shady Oaks Park!

Love, Betrayal and Death in Retirement Village!

158 · CHRISTOPHER MEADES

Crooked Director Responsible for Sweet Old Lady's Death!

Abraham turned around and picked up a ruler. He slapped it hard on the desk and stared at the three prime suspects sitting in a row in cold plastic chairs. Billy Bones was on the left, Alfred on the right and dead in the center was Abraham's nemesis, Conrad, staring into space with those glassy blind eyes. That old English bastard! He had to be responsible for this. He just had to. Abraham felt his blood pressure rise. His chest tightened up. It had been tight for months, ever since his wife started gallivanting about town. And now he had another controversy on his hands, as if his home life wasn't in enough disarray, as if his professional career wasn't already on life support. How he longed for his days at the esteemed Cottage Estates, where the residents were well-bred, where they came from family money, where these three retired gangsters wouldn't have had a snowball's chance in hell of ever getting in. If only Abraham had been more discreet in his money laundering, if only he hadn't been so greedy, he would never have had to slum it in a place like this.

Abraham rounded his desk and shot daggers with his eyes at the three old geezers.

Conrad stared back at him, or rather Conrad stared two feet to the left where he assumed Abraham was standing. "My dear chap," he said. "You seem agitated."

Abraham tossed his ruler across the room. It hit the wall with a resonant slap.

"You're damn right I'm agitated. I know you're responsible for this."

"I haven't the foggiest notion what you're talking about," Conrad said. His tone turned to one of feigned concern.

"You know, you should try to relax a little. If you don't, you're going to give yourself a nosebleed. Take a walk in the park. Smell the flowers. Eat a nectarine."

Abraham leaned in until they were nose to nose. His nostrils flared. "There's a reason I didn't turn you in to the police. I'm going to prove you did this myself and when I do, I'll be the hero. My name will be cleared and you'll rot in prison, for all three months you have left to live."

As he spoke, a slight burst of saliva shot out of Abraham's mouth and sprayed in a mist over Conrad. Instantly the bemused smirk vanished from the elderly assassin's face.

"Step back," he said.

Abraham didn't move.

"Step. Back," he said again, slowly this time. His fake English accent shifted from East Cockney to West Anglia and landed square on something resembling a Welsh dialect.

Abraham saw the intensity behind Conrad's blind eyes, the rigidity in his jaw. Suddenly he realized just who he was talking to. He backed away and turned to Conrad's right. Alfred looked as guilty as a cat with a feather sticking out of its mouth. The only resident who even came close to matching Abraham's lofty height, Alfred's eyes avoided contact, his skin glistened with the first showings of perspiration and he and his three-piece suit seemed terribly uncomfortable in that plastic chair. If Conrad weren't sitting right there, Abraham would have launched into a stern interrogation, he would have cornered Alfred alone and interrogated him until sunrise. Only, how do you extract information from a man who can't speak?

He stepped over to Billy Bones. Bones, with his doddering laughter, his bemused expression and his general confusion — he was Abraham's best chance. Abraham leaned in close. His tone softened.

"Billy, you don't need to be afraid of Conrad. You can tell me what happened, tell me why you did it. You don't need to be afraid. I promise I'll look after you."

Bones, who had no idea why he and his classmates had been summoned to the principal's office, didn't hear a single word this tall man said. He took a good long look at Abraham's round skull and said, "You sure got a strange head on you."

Abraham stepped back, defeated.

"You say that every time I see you."

Billy smiled and nodded.

Abraham addressed all three. "I'm going to find out who did this. I'm going to have the orderlies search your rooms, I'm going to have them search Alfred's car."

"It looks like a Christmas ornament, or a dreidel," Billy Bones said.

"You're going to slip up soon and when you do, I'll be waiting. You have to sleep sometime."

"Idle threats," Conrad said.

Billy sat straight upright. "My cousin gave me a menorah when I was twelve. But I told him — I'm not Jewish. It's your dad who converted."

"I will have my day of reckoning," Abraham said.

"All fire and brimstone is what that'll bring you . . ."

"Billy!" Conrad stood up. He extended his cane and walked toward the door. Alfred and Billy Bones followed.

As they reached the doorway, Abraham couldn't help but have the last word. "It's only a matter of time before I prove it was you."

Conrad ground his dentures. He was beginning to lose his patience with this man. A half century ago, when the impetuousness of youth still lingered in his veins, a gangly halfwit like Abraham would never have escaped a confrontation like this alive. But Conrad had a mission to complete and damned if anyone or anything was going to get in his way. He threw his cape over his shoulder and the three elderly assassins exited the director's office. They walked a safe distance down the hall before he stopped his associates. Conrad curled his gloved hand into a fist.

"This ends tonight," he said.

 twenty-one

At 8:53 p.m. that evening, Henrik arrived at the address on the card to discover what turned out to be a restaurant. He entered the restaurant and was greeted at the door by a 25 Dates employee. This woman wasn't the same one Henrik met on the street, but she was just as beautiful and equally as bubbly. He paid his forty dollars and headed inside. Henrik was stunned by what he saw. There were twenty-five women sitting in the far corner. His eyes drifted to the other side of the room where a near equal number of men had congregated. Henrik felt cheated. He wasn't going to be unique at all! This was some sort of bizarre sex party of which he wanted no part. It was one thing to have sex with twenty-five different women, but it was an entirely different thing to participate in a gross, sweaty orgy. Henrik wanted his forty dollars back.

He looked around for the woman who took his money but she was nowhere to be found. Furious, he sat down in the corner with the other men and waited for her to appear so that he could demand his money back and declare her an even more vile pervert than that old man in the retirement home bathroom.

In the seat beside him, someone was crying. Henrik looked over and was astonished to see that same young man who'd been thrown out of his office building and later came into the hospital with the elderly patient who'd been blown to smithereens. The other men had purposely sat far away from him because he was bawling out loud, occasionally slamming his fist on the table and generally making an uncomfortable scene. Henrik tapped the young man on the shoulder. "Why are you crying?"

Roland looked at him with distraught eyes.

"I lost my job," he said. "I lost my girlfriend and I lost all my friends. Then my grandmother spontaneously combusted."

"Spontaneous combustion? Is that even possible?"

"Apparently."

"Why did you lose your job?" Henrik said.

"Because I'm an idiot."

"And why did you lose your girlfriend?"

Roland brought his hands up and rubbed his eyes. "Because I'm shallow."

"Have you tried getting her back?" Henrik said. "I hear that sometimes when men lose girlfriends, there's a technique for getting them back."

"It's called groveling."

"Yes, that's it. Have you tried groveling?"

"No, not yet."

"Do you think it works?"

"Maybe," Roland said. "I don't know. Who cares?"

Henrik was confused. "Why would you come to this orgy if you were having such a bad day?"

"I came because I already lost four million dollars today. I couldn't stand to lose the forty bucks I paid for this as well."

"So then it's as I feared," Henrik said. "The money is nonrefundable."

"I don't even know how I'm going to talk to these girls," Roland said.

"You have to talk to them first?"

"Yes, you talk to them for three minutes and then you decide if you want to go on a date with them."

Henrik couldn't believe his bad luck that in his first attempt at finding love, he'd inadvertently paid to attend an orgy that involved a great deal of talking. He glanced across the restaurant. "But I can't talk to these women," he said. "I'm simply not prepared."

"Try to get as many phone numbers as you can," Roland said.

In the corner, a bell rang. The 25 Dates employee reappeared and led the participants in a group cheer. As the cheers faded, the 25 Dates employee read a list of rules for the event. She ran around the room and placed numbers on everyone's shirt and before Henrik knew it, the speed dating session had begun.

Conversations got underway immediately. Tension akin to that of a high school dance hovered in the air. It filled each dater's posture, channeled through their bodies and burst unrestrained from the pauses between words. The walls teemed with electricity.

Henrik sat down at his assigned table across from a woman with incredibly large shoulder muscles who proceeded to tell him a slightly funny, slightly frightening story about the time she put a man in a headlock for grabbing her ass in a bar. Henrik waited to speak and when she was finally done, he told her that he would never grab her ass in so much as a cocktail lounge without her express verbal permission. He felt quite pleased with his response. Not only was it accommodating and polite, but from his perspective it bordered on modern-day chivalry. The woman, however, didn't seem impressed. She sneered and launched straight into a second story about a man who rightfully deserved to be placed in a headlock but through sheer luck and social circumstance would likely never receive the uncomfortable roughhousing he had coming.

Henrik had just started to clue in to the fact that she was talking about him when the bell rang. He moved to the adjacent table to start the next date. This woman didn't seem at all impressed when he sat down. Henrik shook her hand and, remembering Roland's advice, promptly asked her for her phone number.

"Aren't you a little too old to be here?" she said.

Normally Henrik would have been so demoralized by that question he would've placed his tail between his legs and run home to eat an entire container of Oreo ice cream. But two tables away was the most beautiful woman Henrik had ever seen in real life. She had wide, round eyes and lips shaped like a tiny red heart. He couldn't wait to talk to her and not even this woman's rampant ageism could dampen his spirits.

Eight and a half minutes later, Henrik finally sat down at the table with the beautiful woman. He forgot all about the matchmaker's rigid rating system and did his best to seduce this incredible creature.

It would have gone so much better if she wasn't completely insane.

"Hi, my name's Henrik."

"I'm Jessica," she said. "But you can call me Evil Jessie."

"Evil, you say?"

"Yes, I'm evil."

Henrik immediately became afraid of this woman. No other person in his entire life had ever been brazen or candid enough to divulge their sinister inner workings to him, let alone insist that evil be part of her name. A single drop of nervous perspiration formed in his left armpit.

"Question for you," she said. "Do you rollerblade?"

"No."

"That's good. Because only gay guys rollerblade."

"Isn't that an offensive stereotype?" Henrik said.

"That doesn't mean it's not true. Do you see that guy over there?"

Henrik looked over to see Roland with his head down on the table, whimpering and rubbing his eyes as some poor woman tried to get him to discuss his three favorite movies.

"He probably rollerblades," Evil Jessie said.

This woman made him so nervous that Henrik started to wonder whether or not she was truly insane. The longer Jessie spoke, the more Henrik started to believe that the mentally deranged, at least those defined as legally crazy by a governing medical body, should be required to wear buttons, or at the very least medical alert bracelets engraved with the specifics of their condition, in order to preclude them from speed dating. It took all his power not to suggest this out loud. After the bell clanged, Henrik walked over to the next table. Evil Jessie seemed to have forgotten all about him as he overheard her telling the next guy that she was positive playing water polo will give you a venereal disease.

Henrik sat down across from a lovely Egyptian woman who, in rapid-fire succession, proceeded to tell Henrik about her job, her apartment, her three cats, her broken wrist at age fourteen, her ex-boyfriend Rob who never understood her and her preference for men with sandy blond hair. She then looked at him for all of five seconds and then said, "So, tell me about yourself."

Up until this point, Henrik had been able to slip through these brief three-minute dates without having to recite anything akin to a monologue. He was now expected to drone on for, at minimum, ninety seconds on subjects that interested him. Moreover, he was probably expected to interject a subtle subtext along the way, extolling his own exceptional qualities in the hope he was memorable enough that this woman might look past their obvious discrepancy in looks and decide to allow him, out of all these men, to bed her.

Henrik wanted to run away and hide. He opened his mouth to speak but only dry air came out. Henrik began to feel faint. Just as he was about to be overcome, the clock proved merciful. The bell clanged and Henrik moved on without saying a word.

He barely had time to compose himself before the next three-minute date started. Henrik sat down across from a mildly unattractive woman wearing a revealing top that prominently displayed her breasts. Henrik suspected that if he looked close, he could see a hint of nipple protruding from her low-cut V neck. For fear of getting caught, he refrained from even a cursory glance.

"My name's Penelope and I'm a Buddhist," she said. "But I live my life through the principles of Scientology."

Henrik glanced around to see if there wasn't some master clock counting down the seconds until this date was over. "Isn't Scientology a religion?" he said. "Aren't Scientologists and Buddhists separate things?"

"Actually, that's a common misconception. Scientologists

can belong to other religions as well. Have you read *Dianetics?*"

"No, not recently."

"Perhaps you should."

"Lately I've been learning a lot about Nanak," Henrik said.

"Nanak? Isn't he the founder of Sikhism?"

"I believe so."

"But you're white."

Henrik looked down at his hands to confirm he was indeed Caucasian.

"Are you saying Buddhists can be Scientologists, but white people can't be Sikhs?"

"Yes," she said.

Henrik searched for that clock again.

Penelope leaned back in her chair. Her plentiful cleavage swelled to the rafters. "So are you religious or not?"

Henrik suspected this question might be a trap. The more of these dates he participated in, the more it seemed to him that evil and trickery were the defining characteristics of these sexual deviants. Penelope was still waiting for an answer. The clock wouldn't ring in time to save him. Henrik had to come up with something. He couldn't lie; she would see right through him. He also feared that were he to answer incorrectly, Penelope might threaten to put him in a headlock. He chose his words carefully.

"I'm not religious, per se. But I believe I have the potential to be quite pious."

Penelope churned her jaw and shook her head. She promptly excused herself to go to the washroom. Thirty seconds later, the bell rang and a five-minute break was announced.

After the break, Roland sat down at the next table and immediately placed his head on the surface and began sobbing uncontrollably. He felt a hand on his arm, comforting and warm. Roland looked up with pleading eyes and was met face-to-face with the most startling creature he'd seen in his entire life. Sitting across from him was a beautiful woman with striking cheekbones and captivating eyes. She had a warm smile and, from what Roland could tell, an athletic figure hiding beneath the table.

But above those captivating eyes lurked a ghastly collection of eyebrows. Earlier that day at the old folks' home, Roland thought he'd seen the epitome of wild, uncontrolled eyebrows. This woman looked like *60 Minutes'* Andy Rooney. The thick, multicolored strands on either side of her forehead were like log cabins that had collapsed and now lay in piles of rubble. At one point, as the woman described her ideal date — a romantic dinner followed by a moonlit walk along the beach — Roland thought he saw one of her eyebrows move — not just side to side; it slithered serpent-like, as though her eyebrows were snakes that had escaped from Medusa's head. Roland stopped crying and gave her a look of bizarre curiosity.

"I feel we have a good connection," the woman said without Roland ever speaking a word.

The bell rang.

"I'm going to check you off as a yes on my little sheet," she said. "Don't forget to check me off too."

Roland would have rather had an electric eel shimmy up his rectum.

"Um, okay," he said.

By the time Roland started his next date, his tears had

pretty much abated. He sat down across from a redhead wearing a Coldplay T-shirt. The redhead had green eyes and her long scarlet hair was braided like Princess Leia's in *The Empire Strikes Back* — not the giant kaiser-roll buns on either side of her head from the original *Star Wars*, but the wraparound loop Carrie Fisher wore in the sequel.

The bell rang and instead of burying his face in his arm and bawling hysterically, Roland decided to give this speed dating thing a shot. After all, what did he have left to lose?

"Let's see here," Roland looked down at the sheet 25 Dates had provided with conversation starters. "My name's Roland," he said. "I'm a business analyst, or rather I was a business analyst. I'm currently unemployed." He glanced at the sheet again. "My favorite movie is *Heat* starring Al Pacino and Robert DeNiro. My least favorite movie is *Ferris Bueller's Day Off*. It's not that bad a movie I suppose, it's just that people talk about it like it's the next *Citizen Kane* and yet every time it comes on TV, I'm bored out of my mind."

The woman hadn't said anything yet, so Roland kept answering questions off the sheet.

"I suppose I like long walks on the beach. Hmmm. What kind of music do I like? Mötley Crüe and Guns N' Roses. You know, the really cool stuff that was popular before those grunge bastards ruined everything."

The redhead stared at him in disbelief.

"Don't you recognize me?" she said.

Roland looked her up and down. He shook his head. "Nope."

"I'm Tamara. You know, Kara's friend? You've met me at least five times. Two months ago you came over to my place for dinner."

"Really? What did we have for dinner?"

Tamara placed her hands on her temples and rubbed them in frustration.

"I made chicken with udon noodles."

Roland's eyes widened. "Oh yeah. Don't you have a boyfriend or something?"

"We broke up," she said.

"How come?"

"Well, not that it's any of your business, but I found out he got a lap dance at some strip club."

"How much did it cost?"

Tamara's eyes turned into flaming red spheres.

"I don't know. Fifty dollars."

"I can see why you were upset," Roland said. "There's definitely more touching involved in a fifty-dollar lap dance than in one that costs twenty bucks."

"Well, thank you for sharing," she said.

Roland glanced up at the clock.

"What are you doing here?" she said. "Where's Kara?"

The bell rang and Roland stood up without answering. He waved goodbye to the scowling redhead and moved on to the next table.

Nine minutes, three dates and one encounter with Evil Jessie later, Roland was once again a complete mess. On top of everything this tragic day had thrown at him, Roland now feared that he might have gotten a venereal disease the last time he played water polo. He wondered why he ever came to this event when it would have been so much easier to curl up in the fetal position in bed and whimper for hours, or better yet sit in a running car with the garage doors shut and let the engine fumes gently purr him to sleep.

When the bell rang, the men stood up to move to the next three-minute date. Roland found Henrik waddling between tables.

"Do you want to get out of here?" he said.

"Where would we go?"

Roland wiped his nose on his sleeve.

"To the happiest place on earth."

Henrik was immediately intrigued. He couldn't help but wonder — what was this happiest place on earth and why had it taken him forty-two years to be invited to it?

Henrik had been through nearly twenty three-minute dates, some memorable, others completely forgettable, still others harrowing to where he feared they might leak into his dreams. He didn't know if he could go through with the rest of them. This orgy had turned out not to be an orgy after all, but a case-by-case assessment of his alpha-male skill set, and Henrik feared he'd failed miserably. Ever since he was a little boy, Henrik had heard stories of how amazing love was and how it made you feel like a special person who really mattered to someone. He decided he wasn't ready for love yet and even if he was, he would never find it here among these evil rollerblade bigots and sexual deviants.

Henrik followed Roland out the doors.

They were headed to the happiest place on earth.

twenty-two

Roland and Henrik hopped in a taxicab and traveled to the seediest area in town. From inside the taxi, Henrik could see junkies shooting up and starving people roaming the streets. This looked entirely different from the utopian society Henrik had imagined. They exited the cab directly across from an old abandoned police station and together entered a bar called the Number 5 Orange. The inside of the club was filled with purple lights and smoke. Henrik noticed immediately that this club was almost entirely populated by men sitting around drinking beer. The only exceptions were the ten or so scantily clad women slinking around in lingerie, asking men if they wanted to dance. Almost every time the women asked, the men turned them down. Henrik couldn't imagine why these men were turning down women for dances.

He and Roland took their seats next to a giant unoccupied stage with a pole in the middle. A woman with enormous fake breasts and long red fingernails leaned into Roland's ear and asked him if he wanted a dance. Roland looked her up and down and then shook his head. He turned to Henrik and said, "I'm going to wait until a better one comes along."

Henrik suddenly realized why this was the happiest place on earth. Inside this club, the laws of the universe were entirely reversed. In here, the men didn't seek out the women. The women sought out the men. Henrik thought to himself, *What great luck I have that on the night I decide to get a girlfriend, I've come to a place where women have to proposition me and not the other way around.*

A woman in a cheetah costume approached the stage and "Pour Some Sugar on Me" by Def Leppard blared over the club stereo. She danced around and took off her clothes while everyone cheered. Henrik was admiring the awesome '80s rock when he looked around for the smiling faces on all the men. There were none. When the men weren't cheering, their faces were deadly serious and even a little glum. Henrik didn't understand. If the Number 5 Orange was the happiest place on earth, why wasn't anybody smiling?

The woman in the cheetah costume finished taking off all of her clothes to "You're Still the One" by Shania Twain and then left the stage. Everyone applauded and bought more drinks. Roland started to cry a little. Henrik looked around at all the glum faces and wondered if the other men were about to cry as well. He started to curse himself for coming here. Entering this bizarro world wasn't going to make him unique. And this most definitely *was not* the happiest place on earth. It was a place of misery and sin and while Henrik regarded these qualities to be distinct (and even admirable) attributes within a single individual, he was not in favor of an entire society based upon them. Moreover, the misery and sin seemed to spread through this crowd like a virus, blurring individuality and deadening these men's souls. Henrik stood to leave when from the corner of his eye, the woman who kissed him at the hospital took the stage in a skimpy schoolgirl outfit.

The past twelve hours had been exceedingly difficult on

Bonnie. Everywhere she went — the coffee shop, her friend's place, the back door of this house of ill-repute — she expected Clyde to jump out from behind a corner and strangle her with his bare hands. Now though, she had to do her job and it was likely to turn her into a living target. Bonnie climbed on stage and waved to the patrons. She surveyed the crowd to make sure her husband was nowhere to be seen and then proceeded to shake her groove thing to Bon Jovi's "Bad Medicine" while keeping one eye glued to the door. In the purse she'd brought to the stage was her small pistol in case Clyde came in. As the song ended and she removed her bra, the club's front door opened. Bonnie leaned toward her purse to grab her gun only to see three old men walk in through the entrance. One was wearing a cape.

Bonnie breathed a sigh of relief and continued dancing to Tears For Fears.

From their table in the second row, Roland wiped his eyes and looked up to see the dancer. To his utter amazement, it was the woman he'd bumped into at the lottery kiosk — the very one who'd taken his winning ticket! Roland grabbed Henrik by the shoulders and shook him.

"Do you realize who that is?" he said.

Yes, Henrik thought, the memory of Bonnie's marshmallow-flavored tongue still fresh in his mind.

In the distance, Billy Bones sidled up to the bar and ordered a Scotch on the rocks. He handed the bartender a crisp one-hundred-dollar bill and told him to keep the change. Billy surveyed the scene. Nearly a dozen women in various states of undress were sashaying through the crowd. Billy's eyes spread wide like the tide as he gazed from G-string to fishnet bra. He downed his Scotch in one gulp and rubbed the pug dog cheeks on either side of his face.

From across the room a Spanish beauty dressed as Supergirl headed in his direction. A wide transparent S was spread across her chest and her daring short red skirt carried high with a hint of blue panties underneath. Poor Billy Bones, having just that afternoon entered a stage of dementia in which he couldn't remember his own name, didn't recognize her at first.

"Bones!" she yelled over the music. "It's good to see you again."

He gave her a confused look.

"It's me, Rosalina Estranova."

Billy Bones looked at her Supergirl costume and scratched his head like a frumpy monkey.

"Your true love!" she said.

Suddenly the memories came rushing back — the Second World War, that bunker he hid in for three days while the Germans stormed overhead, Rosalina's warm touch, her hypnotic brown eyes, that lost weekend they spent naked with a bottle of bourbon and a stash of opium.

"Rosalina!" He wrapped his arms around her.

"Would you like to go upstairs for a private dance?" she said.

Billy Bones glanced over at Conrad and Alfred. He wasn't quite sure who those two men were anymore.

"It would be my pleasure," he said.

Rosalina Estranova, the granddaughter of his true love, took Billy Bones by the hand and led him upstairs where a delighted, delirious Billy spent his remaining portion of the forty thousand dollars on a single lap dance.

At the other end of the bar, Alfred had Henrik in his sights. Conrad stood beside him calmly puffing on a cigarette while Alfred prepared his crossbow for a fatal strike. He was just waiting for Conrad to give the order.

Roland's tears suddenly disappeared. He stood up to ask the woman on the stage what she'd done with his lottery ticket and in doing so, blocked Alfred's clean shot at Henrik. Roland banged his fist on the stage but Bonnie wouldn't look at him. She was too busy staring at the front door, waiting for Clyde to barge in and kill her.

Across the room, Conrad leaned in to Alfred's ear and said, "Take him out."

Concealing the crossbow with his jacket, Alfred moved covertly toward the bar in search of a clean shot at Henrik. He had him in his sights once again.

"Where's my ticket?" Roland screamed at the dancer.

Bonnie finally looked his way. She recognized Roland from the lottery kiosk at the marketplace. "I don't know what you're talking about," she said.

"Listen, you slut . . ."

Henrik stood up and grabbed Roland by the arm. After his kiss with Bonnie, Henrik's mouth had tasted like cherries and butterscotch for hours. That kiss was the only special thing that had ever happened to him. The rest of this world was full of *cottaging* perverts, orgy parties and depressed drones watching women take off their clothes. That woman up there — whose name Henrik didn't even know — was the only one who had ever made him feel special. She'd given him a single pure moment of inimitable distinction and he wasn't about to let this depressed maniac talk to her like that.

Roland struggled to push Henrik away and together the two of them knocked over a pitcher of beer.

From their position at the doorway, a couple of overzealous bouncers stormed over. They had wide Barry Bonds–like heads and biceps as big as Hulk Hogan's. Together they grabbed Henrik and Roland, picked them up like trash bags and carried them in headlocks towards the front door. As they were thrown out into the street, Henrik stumbled onto the sidewalk just in time to see that same outraged Dunkin' Donuts employee from the hospital enter the Number 5 Orange. He had an arrow stuck in his chest and a gun in his hand. Henrik looked over at Roland, who was incensed with him for interrupting his conversation with the dancer.

From inside, they heard a woman's scream and then the emptying of a gun barrel.

The bar patrons poured out into the street in panicked flight. At least sixty men took off in random directions to seek cover. Roland figured out immediately what had happened and started to cry, fearing he would never see his prized ticket again.

Henrik heard two strange sounds, like swords cutting through air. He ran to the doorway to see the Dunkin' Donuts employee stumble out of the bar. Clyde had two more arrows sticking out of him, one in his left shoulder, the other in his right thigh.

"What's your name?" Clyde coughed up a little blood.

"Henrik Nordmark."

"You probably thought you were going to be her new boyfriend," Clyde said. He checked the barrel of his gun only to find it empty. "You're next," he pointed the empty gun at Henrik. Clyde staggered across the street and climbed inside a red Honda Civic with a scratched car bra. He squealed his tires and made a successful getaway.

Henrik looked inside the deserted bar. The only movement was the flash of a crimson-lined cape escaping out the back door. In the center of the stage with her schoolgirl's costume partially discarded, Bonnie lay still and quiet, blood flowing freely from her back. Henrik had never seen such a sight. There was no question. Bonnie was dead.

 twenty-three

In the middle of the night, Bonnie's dead body was brought to the municipal morgue where a young mortician's assistant stripped off the remnants of her schoolgirl costume. The mortician's assistant dutifully removed Bonnie's short plaid skirt and her clunky stripper boots. As she went to remove Bonnie's fishnet stockings, the assistant noticed a small piece of paper taped to the bottom of the dead woman's foot. Gently, she peeled off the paper and discovered it was a lottery ticket. The mortician's assistant glanced around the empty morgue. She was alone. Without giving it much thought, she tucked the lottery ticket in her pocket and continued her work with the body. She jabbed a tube into Bonnie's stomach with a little more delight than usual.

Two hours later, after her shift ended, the mortician's assistant was driving her tiny blue 1967 VW Beetle down the highway when she spotted a Chevron gas station. Chevron was the best gas station in the whole city, she'd decided, because several times a week they brought in fresh cookies from a bakery. She'd had such a stressful day that only a Smarties cookie would suffice. The mortician's assistant pulled over and entered the gas station. To her dismay, the pastry case was utterly devoid of Smarties cookies. She looked at the last few stale biscuits and felt herself about to cry. Begrudgingly, she selected the chocolate chip cookie with the highest chip-to-cookie ratio and approached the counter to pay for it. The mortician's assistant was halfway out the door when she remembered the ticket in her pocket. She handed it to the cashier and took a big bite of her cookie.

The lottery machine played a MIDI-version of the song "We're in the Money."

"You won," the stunned cashier said.

The mortician's assistant shoved half the cookie in her mouth.

"How much? Two dollars?"

"No. Four million."

Kara almost choked to death on her cookie.

Henrik spent a sleepless night struggling to come to terms with Bonnie's death. Before the police arrived, he fled in the opposite direction of Roland, who now seemed to dislike Henrik as much as it was humanly possible to do so. Henrik felt himself close to tears for the first time since he struggled to write that poem.

In his search for self-realization, he'd only pictured death in abstract terms. It had been a theoretical notion and one that always seemed so far off in the future that it wasn't even all that frightening. Now that he'd seen death close up, he was very afraid. He didn't know what to do or who to talk to. He tried to call Parminder to hear more about Nanak but that Betty Sue woman answered the toll-free number again and informed him that no one named Parminder worked in their office. To test whether or not she was lying, Henrik said he desperately wanted to purchase an Ab Lounger Deluxe and when she hesitated, he called Betty Sue a liar and demanded to speak to Parminder immediately or else he would hang up the phone and call the handsome and heroic Chris Hansen from *Dateline NBC* and order him do a revealing exposé on how the disingenuous Christian cable networks outsource their phone centers to India where Sikh people are forced to work for crappy wages.

Betty Sue told Henrik to fuck off and hung up.

Henrik threw his telephone against the wall and stomped around his apartment like a madman, incensed that not only had all his efforts failed to lead him any closer to becoming unique, but in addition, he'd neglected the entire time to examine death and the absolute finality of it all.

To Henrik, the end of his life would be like the fate of the *Titanic* on that April night of 1912. The iceberg had been struck and the ship was going down. Some of the passengers had escaped onto lifeboats, but of those destined to perish, Henrik could never have found purpose the way those brave men in the vessel's bowels did by stoking the engine's fires to keep the power on until the very last moment. Henrik should have been content to have been one of those courageous souls. Yet what he wanted more than anything was to be noble: inspired and inspiring in the face of the infinite black void, much like the violinist in the string quartet who played on as the ship floundered. Steadfast, the violinist's melodies sprayed out into the air, the last gasp of an artist dripping blue into the midnight sky. Henrik would have given his left arm to go down like that.

He could never hope to be first violin, not second violin or even the viola player. Henrik would have been lucky to have been the cellist, droning unnoticed in the background, eddying into the water's black abyss while being completely disregarded by the panicked passengers, the masterful violinists and even by himself.

Henrik yelled out loud. His chest filled with adrenaline. He yelled again.

He stomped his feet and crashed into walls until his neighbors on all sides told him to shut up and go to bed.

The next morning, Conrad, Billy Bones and Alfred met over breakfast at the retirement home. Conrad had woken up in a particularly surly mood. For days, he'd been growing increasingly frustrated with their inability to murder that devious super spy. He declared that by sundown tonight, they would either kill Henrik Nordmark or die trying. Alfred didn't like this idea at all. He scribbled down his objection on a piece of paper and handed it to Conrad, who in turn told him that he was blind and could no longer read. Alfred showed the paper to Billy Bones and motioned for him to tell Conrad what it said; only Billy Bones had lost most of his cognitive brain functions and completely ignored anything put in front of him, with the notable exception of the twenty-six-year-old nurse's breasts.

"Damn that Machiavellian man with his trickery and cunning," Conrad said, referring to Henrik.

He stood up from the table and insisted that Alfred and Billy Bones come along with him. From inside Conrad's room, the three assassins grabbed the crossbow and a quiver of arrows. Together they donned long black overcoats and marched down the hall. Alfred thought it strange that they were heading down the east wing rather than toward the main doors. When they arrived at the office door, Conrad whispered in Alfred's ear. Alfred gave him a look of concern, a look which Conrad couldn't see. Conrad whispered again. This time Alfred's expression turned cold. He nodded his head.

The door opened.

A swoosh cut through the air.

The elderly assassins turned and left the premises.

Three minutes later a scream sounded. The receptionist had entered Abraham Arnold's office to finally demand a raise on her weekly paycheck and was shocked to discover the retirement home director's body lying face down on the floor, an arrow sticking straight out of his back. A pool of red had formed on the carpet. Frantically, the receptionist picked up Abraham's phone and dialed 911. Before she could reach the operator, a large bang sounded. The receptionist took cover under the desk and didn't look up again for half an hour.

Outside, Alfred's foot pressed down on the accelerator a second time. The old LeBaron fired a second torrid blast of smoke out its tailpipe. This time the engine roared and the vehicle peeled out of the parking lot.

Conrad, Alfred and Billy Bones were on their way to find Henrik Nordmark.

In the alley behind the Safeway near his apartment, Clyde was crying and slowly bleeding to death. Last night he reloaded his gun and ditched his car before taking refuge here behind a pile of wooden packing crates. Knowing the police would search his apartment and the local hospital, Clyde slept overnight on a stack of phonebooks. The only thing that kept him warm was the torn car bra he'd managed to unhinge from his Honda Civic. During the wee hours of the morning, he dislodged the arrow that had entered his shoulder, but he couldn't unfetter the one from his thigh and the original arrow was still stuck deep in his chest, making it increasingly difficult to breathe.

The wound in his shoulder didn't hurt so much but the arrow in his chest felt like a hundred bee stings and the one in his thigh was like the bites of a thousand hornets.

Clyde wasn't crying over the pain though. He was crying over the loss of his beloved Bonnie. In all his previous attempts to kill her, he'd never once imagined what life would be like without Bonnie. He expected to be gloriously happy once she was finally eliminated. This wasn't the case at all. He found he missed everything about her. He missed the soft skin at the nape of her neck and the gentle caress when she ran her hand through his hair. He even missed the way she used to yell at him and then apologize by saying "I'm sorry you had to act that way" which was not an apology at all but a further indictment of his actions.

"Dear God! What have I done?!" he cried. From nearby, a couple of stock boys were close enough to hear him and Clyde had to keep his wailing to a minimum in order to avoid detection.

He no longer wanted to live. And judging by the amount of blood he'd lost, he would be dead before nightfall. What a joyous death it would be, to be reunited with his beloved Bonnie. But first he would seek vengeance for that kiss he witnessed at the hospital.

Clyde only had one thing left to do on this earth — kill Henrik Nordmark!

When he finally returned to his apartment above the marketplace last night, Roland found a yellow Post-it note attached to his front door. It was from his former supervisor Chad.

Apparently, Chad had given a second thought to some of the things Roland said.

The note read . . .

> *You disrespectful punk! I've been taking Jiu-Jitsu for seven years and I've never once had to lay a hand on anyone outside the dojo. But I'm going to find you and when I do — I'll rip your head off, spit down your throat and grind your balls into a fine paste!*
>
> *Chad*

Roland was a little surprised that Chad had all of that in him.

He cast a nervous glance down the hallway and then entered his apartment. It was just as he'd left it. Clothes scattered across the floor, a half-eaten burrito from last night's dinner on a plate in the kitchen sink, the same beige carpet, same $400 imitation suede couch against the far wall. He closed his eyes and imagined how a millionaire playboy would decorate this space. A giant flat-screen TV would take center stage and behind that would be red lights and a fully stocked bar to chill the mood. The couch would be replaced with a heart-shaped bed decked out in purple cushions and crimson velvet sheets.

Roland opened his eyes and his ordinary, mundane apartment stared back at him. Nowhere was the opulence of his dreams. He tossed his coat on the counter and slumped down into his computer chair. There were three emails waiting for him. The first was a spam message offering Roland a gorgeous Russian mail-order bride at Serbian-level discount prices. The second alerted him to the 20% worldwide death toll incurred by the Influenza Pandemic of 1918 and the 100% chance such a catastrophe will repeat in the new millennium. Only the third message was real. It was from his former colleague Mason.

It read . . .

> Roland, you've ruined my life. I thought we were friends. How could you be so cruel? I don't even want to get even. I just want you to know that I'm really disappointed in you.
>
> Mason

Roland felt like a block of ice had fallen into the pit of his stomach. If Mason had planned some underhanded scheme to get even, if he'd cursed his name from the rooftops and sworn revenge, Roland might have been able to justify what he'd done. But the tone of defeat lurking behind the sans serif font in this email was too much for him to handle. Roland banged his head into the keyboard. He banged it again and fell down in a heap on top of his desk.

There he caught a glimpse of his reflection in the brass penholder his grandmother had given him for Christmas last year. Like a funhouse mirror the metal warped his image, twisted his forehead and elongated his jaw. "Am I the bad guy?" Roland asked out loud. "Was I wrong this whole time?" Roland could barely look at this distorted picture of who he used to be. Moments ago he thought it was impossible to ever feel worse. Now in addition to being buried under mounds and mounds of self-pity, Roland despised himself.

That night he went to sleep with one eye on the door.

The next morning, Roland woke up with a splitting headache. A lethargy overwhelmed him and it was difficult to even move his arms, let alone get out of bed. He ate a bowl of cereal with bits of banana and found it impossible to stop crying. Once he'd finished every last bit of his breakfast, he picked up the phone and called his ex-girlfriend to make amends. She wasn't home so Roland tried her cell number. It rang three times before she picked up.

"Hello?" Kara said.

"Hi Kara, it's Roland." He could barely hear her over the noise in the background.

"What do you want?" she said.

"I've had the worst day of my life," Roland said. "I had the wrong numbers and I didn't win the lottery. I quit my job and alienated everyone at work and then my grand-mother exploded. And now some guy in an orange golf shirt is coming to grind my balls into a fine paste."

"Wow," Kara said. "How terrible for you."

Roland couldn't tell from her tone of voice whether or not she meant that.

"Hold on a second," Kara said. Roland could hear a man's voice in the background. "Just wait right here and we'll walk up and hand it to you," the voice said.

"Where are you? What are you doing?" Roland said.

"I'm at the television studio. There's going to be a pres-entation in the next minute or so."

"A presentation?"

"Yes, a presentation. Listen Roland, you shouldn't be call-ing me anymore. You broke up with me, remember?"

"You're not still mad about that trading up comment, are

you?" he said.

"Oh no, I'm not upset at all."

"Then help me. Tell me what I should do. I'm thinking of jumping out my apartment window."

"But you live on the ninth floor," Kara said. "You'd probably die."

"I know! That's what I'm trying to tell you," Roland said. "I'm thinking about killing myself."

There was a pause in which Roland thought Kara had hung up. "Hello? Hello?"

"Turn on the Channel 5 news right now," she said.

"What?"

Kara hung up the phone without saying goodbye.

Roland labored over to his fake suede couch and sat down in front of the TV. He clicked the remote to Channel 5 just as the news was exiting a commercial. A scattershot of images promoting the next hour's stories flashed across the screen and then a female news anchor in a pink pantsuit appeared behind a desk.

"We go now to our affiliate KPLN for breaking news," she said. "I believe congratulations are in order for one lucky lady today?" The screen cut to a local news studio in which Kara was standing beside a reporter. On her left was a representative from the lottery corporation, one of the same men Roland had shown his losing ticket to just the other day. The lottery official was holding a large novelty check with Kara's name emblazoned on the front and the amount of four million dollars in big black bold letters. That block of ice that had fallen into the pit of Roland's stomach now leaked down toward his toes.

Kara had a big smile on her face. She reached out and

shook the man's hand.

The lottery official handed over the check and a small round of applause sounded in the studio. Then the reporter asked her the important questions — "What are you going to do with your winnings? What do you have to say to all your friends out there?"

Kara appeared to think about it for a moment and then said, "I don't know what to tell you. I guess you just have to realize you can't control the actions of others. All you can do is control your perspective in this world."

The news cut back to that same anchor in her puffy pink pantsuit.

"Well, doesn't that story just warm your heart?" she said. "Now to our local zoo where the beloved orca whale Mika is due to give birth any day now . . ."

Roland turned off the television and staggered to the center of the room. He fell to his knees, let out an agonized wail and wished he was dead.

When Henrik Nordmark awoke the next morning, he felt like a pilgrim who had traveled thousands of miles across barren lands only to discover there was no trace of the messiah waiting for him at the end of his journey. His quest to become unique had left him feeling even more ordinary, even more generic. He closed his blinds and sat in the dark, intending to pine away hopelessly in his apartment all day. Henrik moped for exactly three minutes before he realized he could simply no longer live like this. He couldn't be plain and boring — not for one more day. This contemptible world had cursed him with a tedious, mind-numbing existence of wearisome days and uninspired nights. Since the moment he was born, Henrik had been waiting to die. He just hadn't realized it until now. His journey led him right back to where he started and he didn't have the strength or the courage to embark on another one.

And now Henrik, armed with the realization that for forty-two years he'd done nothing but drearily wait out the end of his days, decided he could wait no longer. He couldn't live another day in a world where no one noticed him, where he hardly took notice of himself. Henrik Nordmark would take his own life.

But first, he would go to the market for one last plum.

 twenty-four

Henrik trudged down the street in a dreary daze, his every step an added torture, his pace mimicking the dismal march of the condemned. He circled the corner onto the street where the market was located. Once inside the market, he dug through the plums with his fingers until he found a truly moist plum, one bursting with thick red juice. He paid the cashier and then walked out onto the sidewalk where he dug his teeth in. Henrik's teeth penetrated the plum's skin and he felt the sweet sappy liquid against his tongue.

He was planning to take two more bites and then step into oncoming traffic when someone screamed his name. Henrik turned around and saw the injured Dunkin' Donuts employee shuffling zombie-like toward him, his uniform stained with blood and a frenzied look of rage in his eyes.

Clyde raised his gun and shot it in the air. The sound of bullets stopped traffic and sent pedestrians fleeing in all directions. Clyde was still too far away to get a clean shot. He fired the gun a second time and screamed Henrik's name.

"Henrik Nordmark! You're going to die!"

Henrik couldn't believe Clyde had found him. He turned to run in the opposite direction only to see three old men in long black coats standing in his way. The one in the center discarded his coat and swung a cape over his shoulder. Crimson satin settled dramatically in the wind. This man had a crossbow in his hands and looked like a supervillain.

Henrik didn't know what to do or where to turn. Instinctively, he looked up, only to see Roland, the young man from last night, standing on the ledge of his ninth-floor balcony.

"Why, God?" Roland cried. "Why?"

It was all happening so fast. Henrik felt as though he was in the center of a surreal dream. He knew from the looks on the faces of those old men that they were coming to kill him because he'd refused to *cottage* with them at the retirement home. The supervillain had handed his crossbow to the tall skinny one and they were within twenty feet now, taking aim.

Henrik turned and looked the other way. The wounded man with the arrows sticking out of his body was directly behind him, only twenty feet away as well.

These odds were too much to overcome. Henrik knew he was about to die. And he didn't run or hide. Rather, staring death in the face, he turned philosophical. He thought to himself, what have I learned? What is the most important thing in this life and why am I here? His gaze shifted to the plum bursting with juice in his hand. One look at that sweet nectar and Henrik finally realized his place in this world. He didn't have to be exceptional. He didn't have to be different. He was put on this earth just to be Henrik — no more and no less — and what Henrik loved most was to drink in the juice of life. He thought *if I'm about to die, I'll die experiencing all of what life has to offer.*

Henrik took a moist, sloppy bite from his plum.

The evildoers advanced.

Henrik had one bite left. He swore to himself that not even imminent death would stop him from living life to its fullest. He was about to place the plum in his mouth when fate intervened. The slippery morsel fell from Henrik's fingers to the ground.

As Henrik bent over to pick it up, all hell broke loose.

Alfred fired the crossbow but missed Henrik by inches and the stray arrow hit Clyde with a fourth and final blow, this one straight in the heart.

Clyde's gun went off as he died, shot Alfred in the chest and killed the old man instantly.

Conrad screamed at Billy Bones to pick up the crossbow, but Billy had been secretly suffering a series of silent strokes these past few days and the sound of Clyde's gun caused Billy's heart to stop. He staggered slightly and then fell over dead into a pile of garbage cans, a silly smile on his face. Undaunted, Conrad got on his knees and picked up the crossbow. He stood up and took an arrow from his quiver. Conrad struggled desperately to reload the weapon.

Henrik had righted himself as well and was standing like a deer in the headlights, watching the bodies fall.

Conrad left his two dead associates behind and screamed out for Henrik to identify himself so he could shoot him with an arrow.

"Goodbye cruel world," a voice called from above.

Henrik looked up and saw Roland about to leap from his ninth-floor window.

Roland in turn saw Henrik and, hotheaded and suicidal as he was, decided to take Henrik out with him. He cursed Henrik's name and then dived off the windowsill — directly toward the short bald man.

Henrik, in a moment of unprecedented inspiration, called to Conrad. "Here I am, sir. Do your worst." Then he stepped aside.

Conrad stepped forward and prepared to fire. "Where are you?" he yelled, his English accent completely forgotten. "Where you at?"

Up above, Roland was suddenly wishing he hadn't jumped. He screamed a bloody scream as he plummeted toward the earth and then crashed head first into Conrad. Both men died instantly. A stray arrow flew from the crossbow and landed inside the market among a stack of papayas.

Henrik stood in the midst of it all, dumbfounded and unscathed.

Twenty seconds passed before the cashier from the market ventured out into the street. Cautiously, the man who'd never taken notice of Henrik before approached. "My God, man," he said. "You cheated death. I watched the whole thing. You cheated death not once, not twice, but three times. They're going to write about you in the newspaper."

"What will they say?"

"I don't know," the cashier said. "I don't make up the headlines."

"But if you did make up the headlines," Henrik said, "what would you write?"

The cashier thought for a while and then said, "*Man Cheats Fate and Escapes Death Three Times.*"

"But what would the newspaper say about me?" Henrik asked.

The cashier thought long and hard.

"It would say that you're one of a kind."

Henrik Nordmark smiled when he heard the man's words. He took the last piece of dirty plum and shoved it in his mouth. Henrik ground his incisors into everything it had to offer. One of a kind? he thought. That sounds anything but ordinary.

Peggy Leung/Lumeo Photography

Christopher Meades lives in Vancouver, British Columbia. In 2009, his short story "The Walking Lady" won the Toyon Fiction Prize at Humboldt State University. Christopher's work has also appeared in journals across Canada, the United States and the UK. One day he hopes to escape his cubicle and live by the beach. His website is www.ChristopherMeades.com. *The Three Fates of Henrik Nordmark* is his first novel.